Teggs is no ordinary dinosaur –
he's an **ASTROSAUR!** Captain of
the amazing spaceship DSS *Sauropod*,
he goes on dangerous missions and
fights evil - along with his faithful
crew, Gipsy, Arx and Iggy.

Join them now in this special, extra-long
adventure – and relive Teggs's first days
as an Astrosaur cadet in the bonus story:
Destination: Danger!

For more astro-fun visit the website
www.astrosaurs.co.uk

Read all the adventures of
Teggs, Gipsy, Arx and Iggy!

RIDDLE OF THE RAPTORS
THE HATCHING HORROR
THE SEAS OF DOOM
THE MIND-SWAP MENACE
THE SKIES OF FEAR
THE SPACE GHOSTS
DAY OF THE DINO-DROIDS
THE TERROR-BIRD TRAP
THE PLANET OF PERIL
THE STAR PIRATES
THE CLAWS OF CHRISTMAS
THE SUN-SNATCHERS
REVENGE OF THE FANG
THE CARNIVORE CURSE
THE DREAMS OF DREAD
THE ROBOT RAIDERS
THE TWIST OF TIME
THE SABRE-TOOTH SECRET
THE FOREST OF EVIL

Read all the adventures of Teggs, Blink
and Dutch at Astrosaurs Academy!

DESTINATION: DANGER!
CONTEST: CARNAGE!
TERROR UNDERGROUND!
JUNGLE HORROR!
DEADLY DRAMA!
CHRISTMAS CRISIS!
VOLCANO INVADERS!
SPACE KIDNAP!

Find out more at www.astrosaurs.co.uk

Astrosaurs

EARTH ATTACK!

Steve Cole

Illustrated by Woody Fox

RED FOX

EARTH ATTACK
A RED FOX BOOK 978 1 849 41400 5

First published in Great Britain by Red Fox,
an imprint of Random House Children's Publishers UK
A Random House Group Company

This edition published 2011

3 5 7 9 10 8 6 4

Text copyright © Steve Cole, 2011
Cover illustration and cards © Dynamo Design, 2011
Map © Charlie Fowkes, 2005
Illustrations by Woody Fox, © Random House Children's Publishers, 2011

DESTINATION: DANGER!
A RED FOX BOOK 978 1 862 30553 3

First published by Red Fox 2008

Copyright © Steve Cole, 2008
Cover Illustration, map and cards © Dynamo Design, 2008
Illustrations copyright © Woody Fox, 2008

Penguin Random House is committed to a sustainable future for
our business, our readers and our planet. This book is made from
Forest Stewardship Council® certified paper.

MIX
Paper from
responsible sources
FSC® C018179

Printed and bound in Great Britain by Clays Ltd, St Ives plc

Red Fox Books are published by Random House Children's Books,
61–63 Uxbridge Road, London W5 5SA

www.**randomhousechildrens**.co.uk
www.**totallyrandombooks**.co.uk

Addresses for companies within The Random House Group Limited can
be found at: www.randomhouse.co.uk/offices.htm

THE RANDOM HOUSE GROUP Limited Reg. No. 954009

A CIP catalogue record for this book is available from the British Library.

For Beau, Ashton and Alfie Clifford

WARNING!

THINK YOU KNOW ABOUT DINOSAURS?

THINK AGAIN!

The dinosaurs . . .

Big, stupid, lumbering reptiles. Right?

All they did was eat, sleep and roar a bit. Right?

Died out millions of years ago when a big meteor struck the Earth. Right?

Wrong!

The dinosaurs weren't stupid. They may have had small brains, but they used them well. They had big thoughts and big dreams.

By the time the meteor hit, the last dinosaurs had already left Earth for ever. Some breeds had discovered how to travel through space as early as the Triassic period, and were already enjoying a new life among the stars. No one has found evidence of dinosaur technology yet. But the first fossil bones were only unearthed in 1822, and new finds are being made all the time.

The proof is out there, buried in the ground.

And the dinosaurs live on, way out in space, even now. They've settled down in a place they call the Jurassic Quadrant and over the last sixty-five million years they've gone on evolving.

The dinosaurs we'll be meeting are

part of a special group called the Dinosaur Space Service. Their job is to explore space, to go on exciting missions and to fight evil and protect the innocent!

These heroic herbivores are not just dinosaurs.

They are *astrosaurs*!

NOTE: *The following story has been translated from secret Dinosaur Space Service records. Earthling dinosaur names are used throughout, although some changes have been made for easy reading. There's even a guide to help you pronounce the dinosaur names on the next page.*

Talking Dinosaur!

How to say the prehistoric names
in this book . . .

STEGOSAURUS –
STEG-oh-SORE-us

CARNOTAUR –
kar-noh-TOR

IGUANODON –
ig-WA-noh-don

DIPLODOCUS –
di-PLOH-de-kus

HADROSAUR –
HAD-roh-sore

OVIRAPTOR –
OH-vee-RAP-tor

TRICERATOPS –
try-SERRA-tops

MEGALOSAURUS –
MEG-ah-loh-SORE-us

BAROSAURUS –
bar-oh-SORE-us

SPINOSAURUS –
SPY-nuh-SORE-us

CRYPTOCLIDUS –
crip-toh-CLYD-us

ALLOSAURUS –
AL-uh-SORE-us

VELOCIRAPTOR –
vel-ossi-RAP-tor

BARYONYX –
bare-ee-ON-iks

DIMORPHODON –
die-MORF-oh-don

PLATEOSAURUS –
PLAY-tee-a-SORE-us

PTEROSAUR –
TEH-roh-sore

PTERODACTYL –
teh-roh-DACT-il

THE CREW OF THE DSS SAUROPOD

**CAPTAIN
TEGGS STEGOSAUR**

ARX ORANO,
FIRST OFFICER

GIPSY SAURINE,
COMMUNICATIONS
OFFICER

IGGY TOOTH,
CHIEF ENGINEER

Jurassic Quadrant

Ankylos

Steggos

Diplox

INDEPENDENT
DINOSAUR
ALLIANCE

vegetarian

sector

Squawk
Major

DSS
UNION OF
PLANETS

PTEROS'AURIA

Tri System

Corytho

Lambeos

Iguanos

Aqua Minor

Geldos Cluster

Teerex
Major

Olympus

TYRANNOSAUR
TERRITORIES

Planet Sixty

carnivore
sector

Raptos

THEROPOD EMPIRE

Cryptos

Megalos

vegmeat
zone

(neutral space)

SEA REPTILE
SPACE

Pliosaur
Nurseries

Not to scale

EARTH ATTACK!

Chapter One

TIME FOR DANGER

"The waiting's over!" cried Teggs Stegosaur, bursting into the metal meeting room. "I've just seen Admiral Rosso in the corridor. He's on his way here right now!"

Teggs was captain of the DSS *Sauropod* – the fastest ship in the Dinosaur Space Service. He had flown, fought and hungrily munched his way through countless galactic adventures, helped always by his brilliant crewmates Arx, Iggy and Gipsy. They were sitting inside the *Sauropod*'s meeting room, and looked as excited as he was.

"Rosso's in charge of the whole DSS," remarked Iggy, the gruff iguanodon engineer. "Whatever he wants, it must be something big."

"I bet he's going to give us a super-top-secret mission," said Gipsy, the stripy hadrosaur in charge of the ship's communications. "Something only we can handle."

Arx, Teggs's brainy triceratops deputy, smiled. "Let's hope we *can* handle it – whatever it is."

The sound of heavy footsteps carried from outside. "We'll soon find out," said Teggs, quickly taking his seat at the head of the meeting table. "Here he comes!"

Admiral Rosso, a long-necked brown barosaurus, pushed inside and peered down at Teggs and his crew through his glasses. "Ah, hello, astrosaurs." He beamed. "Guess what? You're all going to space prison!"

Teggs gulped. "Er . . . have we done something wrong, sir?"

"Yeah, normally we put bad guys behind bars," said Iggy. "We don't go there ourselves!"

But Arx just smiled. "I think Admiral Rosso means he wants us to *visit* a space prison."

3

"Your clever first officer is quite correct, Teggs," said Rosso. "Have you ever heard of a sea-reptile called Zindi Bent?"

"I remember her from the space news," said Gipsy. "She was an inventor, wasn't she?"

Arx nodded. "She invented automatic robbing machines for that bunch of sea-reptile criminals, the Doom-Flipper Squad."

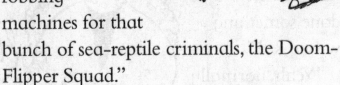

"That's what we believed," Rosso agreed. "The DSS arrested her five years ago. But she has always insisted the Doom-Flipper Squad stole her designs for automatic mining robots and changed them to make machines that suited their own evil ends."

"But she couldn't prove it," Gipsy recalled.

"Which is why she wound up in space prison," said Rosso. "But Prison Governor Bunwinkle has always believed Zindi was innocent. And since her capture, under his watchful eye, she has spent most of her time in the secure workshop, stretching her inventive powers to the limit, trying to create the only thing that can prove her innocence . . . a time machine!"

The astrosaurs stared at Rosso in amazement.

"It sounds incredible, I know. But Bunwinkle assures me she has succeeded." Rosso pressed a button on the meeting table and a TV screen slid up from the smooth surface. He slid a video-disk into its side. "Take a look at this."

Teggs watched as a smart but waterlogged study appeared on the screen. Moments later two nasty-looking yellow cryptoclidus slithered in through the study window and set about a safe with their flippers.

Arx jumped up in his seat. "But . . . they're the ringleaders of the Doom-Flipper Gang!"

"And that is Zindi's study," Rosso informed him, as the robbers on the screen broke open the safe and stole the papers inside.

"Sure enough, they are stealing her designs."

"Then this is the proof that she was telling the truth," said Gipsy. "Why didn't she show anyone sooner?"

"Because this video was taken only a few days ago — by *Governor Bunwinkle himself*!" Rosso turned off the TV with an excited flourish. "Bunwinkle test-drove her machine. He travelled back five years into the past and recorded those slippery villains in the act."

Arx's horns waggled in astonishment. "Then . . . her time machine really works?"

"Come off it!" Iggy spluttered. "I bet that scene was staged somehow. It's all a trick!"

"Perhaps," said Rosso. "That is why I am going to examine Zindi's work for myself."

"It could be the most amazing invention in history," said Arx.

Teggs nodded. "Or the most dangerous."

"A time machine would indeed be a terrible weapon in the wrong hands," Rosso agreed. "That's why I want my finest astrosaurs to guard it – and why I came here to see you instead of telling you over a communicator. I couldn't risk the message being overheard by carnivore spies."

"I'll give the order to increase the ship's speed." Teggs jumped from his seat and ran out of the meeting room. "The sooner we arrive, the better!"

Within the hour, the space prison was looming large through the *Sauropod*'s

portholes. It was a massive castle of
rusting metal, crammed full of carnivore
crooks. As the egg-shaped ship touched
down in the landing bay, Teggs felt an
uneasy prickle travel along his spiky tail.

"I don't see why a time machine is so
dangerous," said Gipsy, joining Teggs,
Iggy and Arx as they walked with Rosso
to the exit.

"If you mess about in the past, you
could end up affecting the future," said
Arx. "Just imagine if Iggy travelled back
to the year his brother hatched and then
accidentally stepped on that egg . . ."

Iggy gulped. "Wimvis would never have been born!"

"And his life would never have happened," Teggs agreed. "You'd have changed history – and not in a good way."

He opened the *Sauropod*'s doors and Rosso led the way outside.

"Aha! There you are." A large and somewhat lumpy grey diplodocus in a white suit waved from the inner door. "I'm Bunwinkle, the governor here."

"Yes, of course." Rosso smiled. "We spoke over the communicator. Funny, you sound different in the flesh."

"I've got a cold," said Bunwinkle, and he sniffed noisily to prove it.

"Did you really travel back through time?" Gipsy asked eagerly.

Bunwinkle looked surprised. "Eh?"

"You took a video camera and recorded the Doom-Flipper Squad," Arx reminded him.

"That bunch of amateurs!" Bunwinkle snarled. "Well, the thing is, I think Zindi Bent was tricking me. I want you astrosaurs to test her machine for yourselves. I've got her chained up in the crew room, ready to begin her demonstration."

"Chained up?" Teggs frowned. "I thought you just proved she was innocent?"

"Look, do you want to test this time machine or don't you?" said Bunwinkle, wobbling off along the bare metal corridor. "Follow me."

"Are you OK?" asked Gipsy. "You look a bit unsteady on your feet."

"I'm fine." Bunwinkle glowered at them.

"I just banged my head this morning . . . on an inmate's nose. Now, keep up!"

"He seems very mean," muttered Gipsy.

"I suppose in a place full of crooks, you have to be," Iggy whispered back.

Suddenly a stegosaurus in a strange helmet and a shirt covered with gold discs burst out through a doorway in front of them. The astrosaurs stared in stunned amazement.

And none stared closer than Captain Teggs . . .

Incredibly – impossibly – the stegosaurus was an identical version of himself!

Chapter Two

THE TIME TEST

"It works!" cried the second Teggs, grinning at his astounded audience. "It actually works!"

"Who are you?" the real Teggs demanded.

But the newcomer ducked back through the door and slammed it behind him.

"Wait!" The real Teggs pushed past Bunwinkle and threw open the door to reveal a long corridor – which was empty. The single door at its far end was shut. "That stegosaurus was a perfect double of me! Where'd he go?"

"Whoever he was, he must be wearing a costume to make himself look like you," Iggy declared.

"Eh? A costume to make him look like someone else?" Bunwinkle rounded on Iggy. "Don't be ridiculous! That could never happen!"

"Then how do you explain Teggs being in two places at once, Bunwinkle?" asked Rosso sternly. "Could your inmates be playing a trick?"

"Your double even *sounded* like you, Captain," said Gipsy.

"I think we should ask Zindi Bent about it." Bunwinkle stomped off on his wobbly legs into the corridor. "Now!"

Teggs and his friends followed the limping governor to the

door at the end. A
strange whirring,
rustling sound
came from within.
Bunwinkle threw
open the door onto
a large, well-lit
room filled with
games and chairs
and TVs. Usually
the prison warders
relaxed here, but
right now there was

just one small sea-reptile inside, her back
turned to them, her body weighed down
with chains. She was sitting fuming
beside a small pyramid-shaped machine
that was covered in switches, screens and
levers.

"So that's Zindi Bent," Arx murmured,
"and that must be her time machine."

"Governor Bunwinkle," said the sea-
reptile crossly. "I don't understand why

you've chained me up like this. You know I'm innocent – thanks to my time machine, you saw the truth with your own eyes, just three days ago!"

"I think you were tricking me somehow," said Bunwinkle. "Now, tell me – did you see an orange-brown stegosaurus come this way?"

Zindi nodded at Teggs. "Only him."

"I'm Captain Teggs Stegosaur," Teggs told her. "This dinosaur looked just like me. He *must've* ducked in here – there's nowhere else he could've gone."

Zindi looked thoughtful. "There is one place he could've gone . . . the future!"

Iggy frowned. "Huh?"

"I knew other dinosaurs would want to test my machine," Zindi explained, "so to demonstrate its power, I've just added a 'send-you-back-five-minutes-in-time' button . . ."

Bunwinkle's eyes narrowed. "Are you suggesting that the second Teggs we saw was the *same* Teggs – visiting from the future?"

"Was he wearing this?" Zindi held up a ridged helmet and a large silver tunic with golden discs stitched onto both arms and up and down the chest.

"Yes!" Teggs stepped forward in amazement. "That's the outfit my double was wearing outside."

"What is it?" Bunwinkle demanded.

Zindi frowned. "What do you mean, what is it? You wore this yourself when you tried out my machine."

"I know that," said Bunwinkle quickly. "I'm only asking so you can explain to our visitors here!"

"Oh. Well, I call it an exo-suit. It protects living things from the powers of the pyramid so they can travel through time safely." Zindi smiled at Teggs. "Looks like the test is going to work – you *are* going to go back in time!"

"Because we've already seen it happen," Arx realized, his horns quivering with excitement.

"Wow, thinking about time travel makes you dizzy! Quick, Zindi, let me put on that exo-suit." Teggs ran over and slipped inside the baggy, tingling material – part costume, part machine. "There!"

"Are you sure it's safe?" Gipsy fretted.

"Don't worry." Zindi pointed to a prominent blue button near the top of the pyramid. "To perform a five-minute time jump, all I have to do is press this. I'll pop your captain into the past for sixty seconds – then bring him back again."

Teggs checked the time on the clock: 18.30. "I'm ready," he said.

Bunwinkle and the astrosaurs watched closely as the machine hummed into life and Zindi hit the blue button. Teggs felt the metal discs on his skin prickle and itch as the world seemed to blur around him . . .

And suddenly only Zindi was in the room – and she had her back to him, absorbed in the workings of her humming, rustling machine. He checked the clock – it now said 18.25.

I really have gone back into the past!
Teggs boggled. Quietly he crept out of
the room. Then he galloped down the
corridor, opened the door and burst
outside. With a mind-spinning thrill, he
saw himself, Bunwinkle and his friends
right there in front of him – just as it
had happened five minutes ago.

"It works!" Teggs cried.
"It actually works!" Then
he dodged back into the
corridor and slammed
the door. He felt dizzy
– Zindi had to be pulling
him out of the past. "So
that's how I seemed
to vanish from the
corridor . . ."
As he staggered back into
the officers' room, he saw the clock was
again showing 18.30. He had returned
to the present, surrounded by his startled
friends – and the grinning Bunwinkle.

"Amazing!" cried Rosso.

"It certainly was," Teggs agreed, taking off the exo-suit. "What an incredible trip."

"Could I see your machine, Zindi?" asked Arx.

"Stuff off, greenie. I'm having it!" Bunwinkle snatched the suit from Teggs. "I've been waiting to be sure this time machine works – and now I know it does, I'll take it!"

"What?" Teggs turned to the burly governor and saw him shrugging off his uniform – to reveal a big zip running down his middle, and another about his neck.

"That's not Bunwinkle's real skin!" Gipsy's head crest had flushed blue in alarm, and Zindi's eyes were on stalks. "It's only a costume!"

"This is a fake Bunwinkle," cried Rosso. "An impostor in a diplodocus suit!"

Arx frowned. "But then ... who's inside?"

"Take a look," came a chillingly familiar voice, as "Bunwinkle" unzipped his neck and pulled off his head – to reveal a scuffed, scarred and tiger-striped velociraptor! He wore a black combat suit. A patch covered one eye. And now he reached down inside his costume and pulled out a gun.

"We've got to be seeing things." Teggs stared in horror. "It can't be you!"

"It's me all right, Teggs," hissed the raptor. "Your deadliest enemy – General Loki!"

Chapter Three

PLOTS AND PLANS

"What are we waiting for?" growled Iggy. "Let's get that stripy loser."

"Stay back, Iggy," Admiral Rosso ordered. "He's holding an atom gun. It could zap us all to ashes."

Teggs raised his spiky tail and bunched his fists. "Where's the real Bunwinkle, Loki?"

"Lying down in a cupboard in his office," hissed Loki. "I trust you'll agree, my impression of him has been superb."

"You ruthless raptor, how did you get here?" Rosso demanded.

"He was a prisoner, like me," said Zindi, still staring in shock. "Locked up in the cell next door."

"And it was you who put me here, astrosaurs," hissed the scuffed, scaly figure. "Me, Loki – commander of the seven fleets of death! Ruler of the meat mines of Raptos! Killer of kentrosaurus, dominator of dream crystals—"

"And smelliest toilet-breath of the year winner ten times over," Teggs concluded. "How in space did you get hold of a diplodocus costume?"

"Simple." Loki smiled. "Two days ago, I bit one of my warders, who sent me to Bunwinkle's office. The governor was just calling Rosso to arrange your visit to Zindi. But his trip through time had left him so distracted I was able to overpower him the moment he hung up! Then I used his private phone to

summon a raptor assault squad – and to
call a fancy-dress shop . . ."

Rosso bobbed his head forward.
"So you could hire a grey diplodocus
costume."

"Precisely," Loki agreed. "I forced
Bunwinkle to act normally and hid out
in his office till my secret delivery arrived
this morning. Perfect timing for Zindi's
wonderful demonstration." He snapped
his jaws. "Now I shall help myself to
my dear neighbour's time machine and
destroy you all."

"No!" cried Zindi.

"You can't stop me,"
Loki sneered.

"Then let's see if *I* can!" Suddenly Teggs lashed out with his fist and thumped the one-eyed raptor on the snout. With a squawk, Loki was knocked right out of the neck of his diplo-suit. And as he fell, he dropped the gun.

"Get him!" Teggs yelled.

Arx, Iggy and Gipsy started forward at their captain's command. But then the zip down the middle of the abandoned costume opened up, and a dozen vicious-looking black-and-orange reptiles rushed out with horrible speed.

"Raptors!" boomed Rosso in warning. "Must be that assault squad Loki called in. They've been working that diplodocus costume together, like a jumbo pantomime horse!"

But as the evil reptiles began their attack, Teggs rolled onto his back and spun round, knocking three of them to the floor with a single sweep of his spiky tail.

At the same time, Gipsy scooped up Loki's fallen gun – but before she could aim it, another slavering raptor knocked it out of her grip. Gipsy booted the raptor aside, and it staggered straight into a hefty punch from Iggy. At the same time, Arx butted two raptors over to Rosso, who lumbered forward and squashed them under his huge feet.

Teggs dodged another raptor, leaped over the empty diplo-costume and landed beside Loki – who was lying face down, apparently cowering in fear. "Give it up, Loki. You're finished."

"Finished?" Loki rolled over to reveal that he now wore a gas mask. "You potato-brained plop-head! *You're* finished . . ." He hurled a white cube down at the floor and it burst open in a hissing haze of smoke.

"Gas!" Teggs gasped. "Look out, everyone!" But already his head was spinning. Within moments the world about him had dwindled to darkness, and he knew no more . . .

"Wake *up*, Captain!" Teggs stirred groggily at the sound of Gipsy's voice. His eyes flickered open and he saw her face looking down at him, full of concern.

"It's all right, sir.

You were closest to the gas so you've slept longer than everyone else. But you're going to be fine . . ."

Suddenly Bunwinkle pushed in beside her.

"Get back!" Teggs cried.

Gipsy shushed him. "Don't worry, this is the *real* Governor Bunwinkle, sir."

Teggs breathed a sigh of relief. "I'm glad you're OK. Where's Loki and his assault squad?"

"I'm afraid they got away," said Bunwinkle. "With the time machine."

"Admiral Rosso's gone straight to DSS HQ and put the whole vegetarian sector on red alert," said Gipsy quickly. "We'll find him."

"Not if he's hiding somewhere in the past," Teggs muttered.

"I'm sorry," said Bunwinkle, helping Teggs to stand. "That wretched raptor threatened to have my grandmother eaten if I tried to warn anyone he'd escaped. Then he knocked me out and tied me up. What could I do?"

"It's what *Loki* could have done that worries me." Teggs shook his dizzy head. "He said he'd destroy us all – so why didn't he?"

"I think he wants us to sweat," said Zindi. She was free of her chains now and working with Arx, hunched over a mass of machinery and wires. "He knows that with a time machine, he can strike whenever he wants."

"Loki literally has all the time in the world," said Gipsy sadly.

Teggs looked about. "Where's Iggy?"

"Stoking the *Sauropod*'s engines," Arx

reported, plugging cables into sockets inside a metal frame in the shape of a pyramid. "Admiral Rosso wants us to be ready to go after Loki as soon as Zindi and I have finished here."

Teggs frowned. "And what are you doing?"

"Building an identical time machine from my notes," said Zindi. "It took me five years to build the first one . . . but with Arx's help and supplies from your ship, the second one should be ready in twenty-four hours!"

"Now" – Gipsy turned

to Bunwinkle – "we'd better get back to sewing the new exo-suits . . ."

Teggs saw a heap of silvery material stitched through with wires and golden discs, and a pile of half-finished helmets. "You're making replacements for the safety gear Loki took?"

Bunwinkle nodded. "For you and your three friends to wear when you go after him. It's a good thing I'm the reigning champion in the Space Prison Sewing League!"

Teggs smiled weakly. "It looks as if you guys have everything under control. What should I do?"

"I think you should rest until that gas

has completely worn off, Captain," said Gipsy fondly. "Something tells me we're headed for the greatest adventure of our lives!"

Teggs was too worried to rest. As soon as he'd stopped feeling dizzy from the gas, he went to the *Sauropod*'s gym for a workout. His space radio was tuned in to DSS news reports – Rosso had put hundreds of ships on Loki's trail. If only one of them would find something . . .

Suddenly he jumped as a new report squawked from the radio's speakers. "A raptor assault squad has been arrested while trying to escape in sector seven of the Veg-meat Zone."

"YES!" Teggs cheered.

"Unfortunately," the newsreader went on, "General Loki was not among the captured carnivores."

Teggs groaned. "BOOOOOO!"

"However, a heavily shielded raptor death-flyer *has* been sighted in sector eight." The newsreader sounded grave. "It vanished into a small black hole, believed to be a newly-formed tunnel in space . . ."

"A space tunnel!" Teggs breathed. The *Sauropod* had travelled through one before, and had barely survived. Space tunnels were like intergalactic short cuts between two distant points – a hundred-year journey might take mere minutes by space tunnel. But any such voyage was incredibly dangerous – the forces within the tunnel could smash spaceships to smithereens . . .

Teggs pressed a red button on the radio – the hotline to Admiral Rosso. "Hello?" came Rosso's voice.

"Sir, this is Teggs. Do I have permission to

pursue Loki through that tunnel?"

Rosso paused. "Granted," he murmured. "I was just about to contact you. Our experts have interrogated Loki's gang of raptors and studied that space tunnel they made. And now we know where Loki has gone."

Teggs waited tensely. "Well?"

Rosso took a deep breath. "The space tunnel leads to . . . Planet Earth."

"Earth!" Teggs gasped in awe. "The ancient home of the dinosaurs. But why would Loki want to take a time machine to Earth?"

"None of us know, not even his raptors," Rosso reported. "But you can be sure he has something terrible in mind. Whatever it takes, Teggs – Loki must be stopped!"

Chapter Four

THE DINOSAURS OF MARS

Within twelve hours, the astrosaurs had
waved goodbye to Zindi and Bunwinkle
and were jetting off to the space tunnel
in the *Sauropod*.

Everyone inside was hard at work.

Iggy was busy testing the powerful
force-field generators he and Arx had
installed in each of the ship's six shuttles.

Together they
would create a
super-tough
invisible
shield right
around the
Sauropod.

Arx and a group of iguanodon engineers were checking and double-checking every circuit in the new time machine. "It's an exact copy of the one Loki stole from Zindi," Arx noted. "It's not strong enough to send the whole *Sauropod* back through time, but it should be able to transport a shuttle with a crew of four."

Chirping in agreement, a group of dimorphodon – the *Sauropod's* flying reptile flight crew – flapped around Shuttle Alpha, fitting it with special exo-discs that would keep it safe on the incredible journey ahead.

Meanwhile, Gipsy and Teggs were on the flight deck testing the special exo-suits, snipping at loose stitches and checking that each special disc was in place.

Teggs tried on his own suit. "I shouldn't have eaten those bushes at lunch time!" he groaned, trying to hold in his stomach. "Do we really have to wear these things?"

"If we don't," Gipsy told him, "Zindi said our bodies will be torn apart by raw time energy the moment we try to travel."

Teggs gulped. "We really have to wear these things."

"Warning!" shrieked the alarm pterosaur through speakers around the ship. "Space tunnel dead ahead. Starting to suck us in. SQUAWWWK!"

Teggs looked at Gipsy. "This is it!"

He switched on the scanner screen. Starless blackness gaped ahead of them.

Gipsy switched on her communicator. "All crew stand by for a bumpy ride!"

Arx hurried onto the flight deck and took his seat. "The time machine is ready," he announced. "We can use it as soon as we've travelled through the tunnel."

"Good work," said Teggs. "But are you sure we will be able to find Loki?"

"Zindi built a tracer into her time machine, in case it ever got lost," Arx explained. "Right now its signal shows that Loki has gone back sixty-five million, one hundred thousand and fifty-six years into the past."

Teggs whistled. "That's a long way back."

"But nothing's changed in our own time, has it?" said Gipsy. "Perhaps his ship didn't make it through the space tunnel. Or if it did, perhaps he hasn't been able to do whatever it is he wanted to do."

Arx shook his head. "When an earthquake happens at sea, it creates a tidal wave. It may take many minutes for that wave to strike land, but it hits in the end. And I think a *time*-quake is much the same."

Teggs nodded. "Even now the effects of Loki's meddling – what he'll do

if we *don't* go back and stop him – could be crashing through the centuries towards us . . ."

Iggy's face appeared on the scanner screen. "The space tunnel is pulling us in faster, Captain. Should I put the engines in reverse to slow us down?"

"No, Iggy," said Teggs. "The sooner we're through this thing the better.

Switch on those shuttle shields of yours and increase our thrusters to maximum power!"

"Maximum?" Iggy puffed out his scaly cheeks, then chuckled. "Right you are, Captain."

Teggs turned to Sprite, the dimorphodon's team leader. "Shut down all but the most vital systems."

Sprite launched into the air, tweeting to his fellows as they zoomed and swooped between the controls, pulling levers and flicking switches. Lights winked out and screens went blank as the *Sauropod* picked up speed.

"Entering the space tunnel in five seconds!" Arx shouted.

"Five . . . four . . . three . . ."

Teggs wedged himself into his control pit. "Hold on tight, everyone. Here we go!"

As Arx's countdown concluded, the ship shook and started to spin. The air grew hotter. The few remaining lights glared red like STOP signs. But there was no turning back now. Teggs closed his eyes as the *Sauropod* whizzed onwards through the tunnel, creaking and grinding and rattling and stretching. He thought his bones would bounce right out of his skin as the great ship's flight grew wilder, crazier, completely out of control . . .

Then – WHOOOSH!

Glowing red-hot, the *Sauropod* was

flung out the other end of the tunnel like a sizzling stone.

"Brakes!" Teggs commanded, as dizzy dimorphodon fell flapping all around him.

Arx pulled hard on a big lever, and with a screeching, scorching rush of reverse energy, the *Sauropod* came to a steaming stop.

"Well," said Teggs, clutching his queasy tum. "That wasn't so bad."

"It was completely horrible," said Gipsy. "But at least we're still alive."

43

"Switch all systems on again," said Teggs, climbing out of the scorching-hot control pit. "Did we make it, Arx? Have we come out in Earth's solar system?"

With a wobbly hand, Arx switched on the space radar. "We're just forty million miles away from Earth, sir," he reported. "Close to the planet Mars."

"Wow." Gipsy whistled. "The history books say that the first dinosaurs in space lived on Mars."

"And Venus too," said Arx. "They used up most of the solar system's resources — that's why when the meteor hit Earth, the dinosaurs had to leave this part of space altogether and strike out for somewhere new."

Teggs nodded. "And now, sixty-five million years later . . . we're back!"

"Mars is a dead world now," Arx declared. "The only place around here that can support life is the Earth — and it's full of those funny human things."

44

Teggs nodded. "I've seen blurry pictures taken through megascopes. They're an odd bunch. I hope they don't spot us in space – they'd most likely try to blow us to bits."

"They won't," Arx assured him. "Human technology is pretty basic. They don't even have proper spaceships."

"Then what is THAT?" Gipsy pointed at the scanner, which had just flickered back into life. It showed a huge, scary spaceship approaching; it was shaped like a double fang and a red skull was stencilled on its side.

"Must be Loki's ship," Teggs murmured. "He can't have had a chance to use the time machine yet."

Arx wasn't sure. "Loki took a shielded death-flyer through the space tunnel, remember? I don't recognize this design."

"Probably a new raptor invention." Teggs turned to Sprite. "Steer us around Mars. When Loki follows us, we'll double back and attack."

The dimorphodon clattered away to obey. But then Gipsy gasped. "Message incoming, Captain – from Mars!"

"But I thought it was a dead planet?" Teggs frowned. "Put the message through."

"This is Martian Dinosaur Command," came a low, hissing voice. "Identify yourselves, or our warships will attack."

Gipsy gulped. "Dinosaurs with warships on Mars?"

"Space radar shows there are massive dino-space forts all over the planet," said Arx incredulously. "And loads more on the Earth."

"But what about the humans?" Gipsy quavered.

"Switch on the long-range astro-scopes," ordered Teggs. "Let's have a look at them."

Arx flicked some switches and a blue world swam fuzzily into view. Teggs had seen its picture in history books – now he and his friends gazed out in wonder at the real thing . . .

But as the shuttle's super-telescopes zoomed in on the planet, one thing became very clear.

There *were* no humans on the Earth!

The planet was full of dinosaurs –
meat-eating dinosaurs of many different
breeds. Their filthy cities and meat farms
were everywhere.

'Something is very wrong," Teggs
muttered. "No humans and no plant-
eating dinosaurs. Only carnivores."

"This is Martian Dinosaur Command,"
came the snarling voice again. "You have
been classified as hostile. We will now
destroy you."

"Wait!" said Teggs. "This is an
astrosaur ship on an urgent mission for
the Dinosaur Space Service."

"Astrosaur?" sneered the voice. "What's an astrosaur? And what is the Dinosaur Space Service?"

Teggs tried again. "We've come from the Vegetarian Sector—"

"The what?" Nasty laughter crackled over the speakers. "You'll be telling us you're a ship full of plant-eating dinosaurs next."

"We are!" Teggs shouted. "What's so funny about that?"

"Everyone knows the plant-eaters were wiped out by the great meteor," the voice snarled. "Only us meat-eaters escaped before it hit – and a few thousand years later we came back again."

"What a pathetic attempt to trick us," came another mean-sounding voice. "Don't you know anything about history?"

"Not *this* version of history," said Teggs quietly. "It's been rewritten – by Loki!"

Gipsy's headcrest had flushed pink with shock. "He's started a time-quake sixty-five million years ago, and the aftershocks have destroyed our present! Everything we've ever known . . . all our friends . . ."

"They no longer exist." Teggs could hardly take it in. "So . . . how come *we're* still here?"

"We must have been inside the space tunnel at the moment history changed," said Arx, "and so we were protected."

Teggs gazed out at the terrifying pictures on the scanner. "The last survivors of our own time . . ."

Suddenly the *Sauropod* rocked as carnivore missiles exploded all around.

"We won't survive much longer if we

don't get out of here!" yelled Gipsy.

"Call Iggy and tell him to fire up Shuttle Alpha." Teggs whistled to the dimorphodon leader. "Sprite, take evasive action. Keep those Martian meat-guzzlers distracted while Arx, Gipsy, Iggy and I take the time machine – and get on Loki's trail."

Sprite saluted. "Eeep!"

"Thank you." Teggs gave him a crooked smile as the ship shook once again. "I hope I see you again too." As Sprite chirped out orders to his chittering team, Teggs turned to Arx and Gipsy. "Quickly, you three – grab your exo-suits and let's get to the shuttle bay." He took a deep breath, his heart pounding. "I hope that pyramid's fully charged. Our next stop has got to be Earth – in the distant past!"

Chapter Five

DOWN TO EARTH

"It's going to be a bumpy ride," Iggy told
Teggs, Arx and Gipsy as they bundled on
board Shuttle Alpha. All four were now
wearing exo-suits and ready for action.
"Stand by for blast-off!"

As the *Sauropod*'s exit hatch slid open,
Teggs saw the blackness of space lit
up by streaks of laser fire and
mega-bright explosions
as the carnivore craft
continued their
attack. "Think
you can steer us
safely through
that lot, Ig?"

"The shuttle's force field took a walloping in the space tunnel. But I'll do my best," Iggy promised. "With luck, those Martian meat-chompers won't even notice us go."

"Activating time machine." Arx switched on the metal pyramid that sat at the back of the shuttle, and it glowed red. The gold discs on the astrosaurs' exo-suits – and on the outside of the shuttle itself – began to glow too. "Power building . . ."

A huge explosion just outside nearly knocked them to the floor. "That was close," said Gipsy shakily. "We could be blown to bits before the pyramid has even warmed up."

"So let's find somewhere a little quieter," yelled Iggy, releasing the brake. "Here we go!"

The shuttle shot away. Gripping the flight stick, Iggy steered with fierce concentration, looping the loop around incoming missiles, veering left and right to dodge the barrage of blasts from the carnivore warship . . . Finally Shuttle Alpha broke free of the conflict and zoomed away through the blackness of space towards the green-blue disc of the Earth.

"Well done, Ig." Teggs clapped him on the back and looked down at the pulsating pyramid, which had started to steam. "Arx, how's the time machine doing?"

"Power systems are reaching critical," cried Arx.

"What does that mean?" asked Gipsy.

Arx stared helplessly at the machine. "Either it's about to explode and blow us to bits ... or we're going to make the time-jump!"

Teggs wasn't sure which option was scarier. But the next moment a massive flash of red lightning zapped through his senses. It was a thousand times more powerful than his last little hop through time. The world around him seemed to melt like hot wax. Teggs felt as though he were riding the fastest rollercoaster in the universe, spiralling through the cold infinity of space ...

BLAMM! Again the crimson light-flash shocked through the shuttle, and suddenly everything seemed back to normal.

"First the space tunnel, then the *time* tunnel," Gipsy groaned. "My poor tummy needs a holiday."

"The time machine's power cells have blown a fuse," Arx fussed, waving at a wisp of smoke coming from the back of the golden pyramid. "I hope I can fix it. If I can't, we'll never get back again."

"We can't waste time worrying about that now." Teggs took off his helmet and exo-suit, and his friends did the same. "The important thing is, we made it!"

Through the windscreen, up close, the Earth hung in space like a perfect blue marble.

"Just think," Iggy murmured. "This is the world where dinosaur life began, all that time ago."

"But we don't know much about our last days on Earth," Arx mused, "or the next few centuries for that matter. The records were long since lost . . ."

Suddenly a vast shining shape swooped

56

down out of nowhere.

"Look out!" Teggs yelled.
There was a
wrenching
CLANG! and
a metal spike
tore through
the side of
the shuttle,
missing Gipsy
by millimetres.
Like a mouse
seized by a
supersonic steel eagle,
Shuttle Alpha was snatched away – and
the astrosaurs were flung in all directions.

"Our air's escaping!" Teggs yelled.
"Sealing foam, Iggy!"

"On the case." Iggy was already
squirting special airtight foam over the
hole to seal it.

Gipsy glared at the spike. "What is this
thing?"

"It looks like a primitive probe for absorbing star energy," Iggy told her. "We've been speared by a spaceship!"

"But whose spaceship?" Teggs scrambled up. "Can we talk to them?"

Gipsy was already tapping at the shuttle's controls. "No reply."

"The space satellites that carry our communications didn't exist sixty million years ago," said Arx gravely. "So our communicators won't work."

"Look!" Iggy pointed to the windscreen, which was now completely filled by the seas and continents of Earth. "The ship's coming in to land – and taking us with it."

"It looks like we'll soon be meeting the Earth dinosaurs of this time," Teggs murmured. "But who are they, and what are they like?"

Gipsy swallowed hard as they whooshed through the atmosphere. "Looks like we're going to find out – any minute!"

Skewered like a tiny sausage on a colossal cocktail stick, the shuttle broke through a thick bank of clouds and sailed low over a patchwork land of forests and lakes, hills and plains, winding rivers and snow-capped mountains.

Teggs guessed it was towards one of these mountains that they were headed. He glimpsed hundreds of huts and cabins – some kind of settlement. Then the thick whirls of smoky exhaust blocked his view as the spaceship that had spiked them landed on the mountainside.

Almost at once he heard a loud clunk from outside, and then mutterings and whispers.

"What's out there?" hissed Gipsy. "If only this stupid smoke would clear."

Then a spiky figure in a quilted suit and space helmet appeared at the window. The astrosaurs jumped in surprise. Teggs saw that the figure stood on a platform carried by four stout pterosaurs – a kind of flying taxi. Slowly the figure removed his helmet . . .

To reveal a dark green stegosaurus!

Teggs stared in wonder. Dinosaurs had gone on evolving over the last 65 million years, and this stegosaurus was clearly less advanced. He had no hands as such. His legs were thick and solid, his body was bulkier and his backplates were bigger. He looked a formidable sight – but his smile was warm and friendly.

"Hello," the stegosaurus called through the window. "I'm sorry we crashed into you. We didn't see you. It was like you came out of nowhere!"

Teggs smiled wryly. "I suppose we did a bit. Who are you?"

"I'm Zac Stegosaur – community

61

chief, inventor and adventurer." Zac peered in through the windscreen. "Hey, this is quite a ship you have, Mr . . ."

"Teggs Stegosaur," said Teggs. "And I like adventures too! Open the doors, Iggy." He lowered his voice. "And remember, we can't let anyone in this time suspect we're from the future – if they believed us, it might change history – so act primitive!"

Iggy flicked a switch and the door slid open. Coughing on exhaust smoke, the pterosaurs carried Zac round so

he could climb inside Shuttle Alpha. "Wow, I've never seen technology like this before. Where did you get it?" He frowned thoughtfully. "You look kind of different from other 'saurs. Where are you guys from?"

"Er . . . we're from all over the place," said Teggs. "Iggy built our ship."

Iggy nodded. "Um, yes. With help from Arx and Gipsy, here."

"I'm pleased to meet you all," said Zac. Then he noticed the crumpled spur of metal sticking out through the wall. "Oh no! Look at my ship's energy-probe. Without that, we can't recharge our power systems in space."

"Don't worry, I can soon mend it," said Iggy. "But what about *our* poor ship?"

"Well, I don't mean to be rude," said Zac, "but while this little ship might look flashy, it's not going to take you far from old Earth, is it? Where are your food supplies? Where are your thousand-years' worth of spare parts? It's just too small — you should think about joining us plant-eaters in the *Soar-a-saurus*."

Teggs frowned. "What's that?"

"The last great hope for all veggie dinosaurs to escape Earth before the meteor hits," said Zac grimly. "I just hope we get her finished before *we're* finished. Six months ago, our telescopes picked up the giant meteor headed our way and we've been building the *Soar-a-saurus* ever since."

"How long before the big rock hits?" asked Gipsy.

"You mean you don't know?" Zac stared in amazement. "We have just a day and a half left. In thirty-six hours, the Earth goes *boom* . . ."

Teggs nodded grimly. "And if Loki isn't stopped, we'll all go *boom* with it!"

Chapter Six

CRAFT OF THE FUTURE

"Well, Zac," said Teggs, "I'm not sure we can come with you – but we will certainly help you get your *Soar-a-saurus* ship-shape."

"I can't see at all what shape it is," Iggy complained, peering out through the fading smoke. "But we're a long way up. Are we stuck right at the top of it?"

Zac gave a friendly snort of laughter. "*This* isn't the *Soar-a-saurus*, Iggy. This

is just one of the six tug-ships needed
to tow her out into space." He pointed
through the mist, past the mountain and
into the valley beyond. "Look ... there's
the *Soar-a-saurus*!"

Teggs and Gipsy joined Arx and Iggy
in the doorway – and all of them gasped.
In the distance, a humungous heap of
metal sat wedged between two hillsides
– an angular spaceship as big as a city!
Dinosaurs swarmed over it like specks –
fixing, welding, loading, installing ...

Gipsy boggled. "That thing's
ma-hoosive!"

"It needs to be," said Zac. "It's got to hold thousands of plant-eaters as well as eggs from every species, kept frozen and ready to hatch on distant worlds."

"Now I see why you need six super-speedy space tugboats to drag it out of Earth's atmosphere," said Iggy. "It's so big, it could never take off by itself."

"But it'll get all us plant-eaters away," said Zac fiercely. "You'll see. It will work!"

Gipsy put a gentle hoof on his shoulder. "Do some dinos think that it won't?"

Zac sighed. "The carnivores laugh at us because the *Soar-a-saurus* won't run on clockwork power like every other spaceship."

"Clockwork?" Iggy spluttered. "That's crazy!"

But Arx nudged him in the ribs. "This far back in history, most dinosaur machines ran on clockwork."

"You're right, Iggy, it IS crazy," said Zac. "My idea is to run spaceship engines on dung! By burning dung you get powerful gases that can push a spaceship five times as fast . . ."

"Spaceships that run on dung, eh?" Teggs smiled. "You know what, Zac? I think your idea is going to catch on!"

"The carnivores don't think so. They're all leaving the planet in a fleet of clockwork rockets." Zac pointed through the porthole on the other side of the shuttle. "You can see for yourself – their camp's on the other side of the mountains."

Now that the smoke had faded, the astrosaurs could see clear across the landscape in the opposite direction.

Giant spires of blood-red metal stood hard against the sky – and bolted onto the sides were gleaming metal tubes.

"Um . . ." Iggy lowered his voice. "Is it me, or do those tube things look like laser cannons – *modern* laser cannons, from *our* time?"

"They certainly do," Teggs agreed.

"But the history books say that on Earth our ancestors built no weapons," Arx muttered. "They battled with teeth, tails and claws as they had always done."

"There's only one dinosaur who could stick modern lasers onto ancient rocket-ships," said Gipsy.

Teggs nodded. "General Loki. And we're running out of time to stop him!"

Zac and his four powerful pterosaurs took the astrosaurs down to the plant-eater camp on the rickety platform. Teggs thought of the dimorphodon and the rest of his crew, thousands of miles and millions of years away, trapped in a terrifying future that should never have been.

Hang in there, guys, Teggs thought. *We'll put things right.*

As the platform was whisked through the sky, it offered a good view of the whole camp. Different dino-breeds of all sizes were working together in the fields, gathering a humongous harvest.

Young hatchlings and old dinos were doing their bit, carrying supplies on board the *Soar-a-saurus* or shovelling dollops of dung into the gigantic engines built into the back of the super-colossal craft. Other pterosaurs were helping too, swooping about with things to be packed and passing messages between different groups.

Teggs was glad to see the *Soar-a-saurus* was well defended. The steep sides of the valley helped to shield it, and a tall metal barrier ran along the hills that faced out over carnivore territory.

"That's an electric fence," Zac explained as they glided over it.

"The carnivores used to sneak in and raid our camp, stealing supplies for their rocket fleet. So I designed that to keep them out."

"You're quite the inventor," Arx observed as they came in to land over a field picked bare of all but a few blades of grass.

Zac shrugged modestly and checked his watch. "I'm just trying to make sure we all get out of here before that meteor hits."

"No wonder everyone's working so hard," said Gipsy as they landed in the mud with a bump.

"I'll arrange another flock of pterosaurs to lift your shuttle off our tug-ship and bring it down here," said Zac. "But I'm afraid I can't spare anyone to help you fix it. I need to repair that tug-ship and test out the other five."

"I'll help you," said Iggy, clambering off the platform with his friends. "I'm good with engines."

"And I'm clever with machines," added Arx.

"We'll take any help we can get," said Zac gratefully.

"And in the meantime, I'd better pay a visit to the carnivore camp," said Teggs.

"What?" Zac gasped. "Are you crazy?"

"I *have* to go," Teggs told him. "You see, when you ran into us in space we were on the trail of a bad-news raptor named Loki. We think he's going to try to stop you leaving."

Gipsy turned to Teggs. "I'd like to go with you, Captain. Loki's too tricky to tackle alone."

"He won't be alone," Teggs reminded her. "He'll have thousands of carnivores with him!"

"I still want to come," Gipsy insisted.

"Really, guys," said Zac. "Tomorrow we'll be leaving Earth. The meat-munchers will be too busy preparing for their own rocket-ride to safety to bother with—" He broke off at the sound of a crash from across the field.

Teggs turned and saw that a pretty yellow stegosaurus with little hatchlings tucked between her backplates was trying to pull a heavy crate with her tail.

"Gazell!" Zac's face creased with concern and he hurried away. "Don't try to carry those spare parts by yourself. Let me help you . . ."

"Arx, Iggy, you try to help too," Teggs said. "Gipsy and I will head off to the carnivore camp and do our best to stop Loki – before something terrible happens!"

Two hours later, as the moon hung like a chewed silver claw in the perfect black of the night, Teggs and Gipsy were nearing their destination. Pausing beside a stream, they noticed a large sign, the words scratched into a sheet of metal:

WARNING – Carnivore Camp Ahead.
Plant-Eater Trespassers Will Be Eaten.
Or Scrunched.
Or Splatted.
Or Jumped Up And Down On Until Dead Or Very Unwell.
Then Eaten.

"Do you think they're trying to tell us something?" said Gipsy nervously.

"I think we need a disguise." Teggs crouched

down beside the stream and picked up a couple of sharp stones. He stuck them under his lip so they looked like fangs. "How's that?" he mumbled.

"Those backplates are a dead giveaway," Gipsy informed him. She reached into the stream and scooped out some mud, then smothered it over Teggs's back like brown cement. Soon his spiky back was hidden beneath a smooth ridge of dirt. "Now, if you walk on your back legs ..."

Teggs reared up and offered Gipsy a couple more pointed stones he'd found. Gipsy slipped them in place. "I look like a walrus!"

"Let's just hope no one looks at us too closely," said Teggs. "Try to act like a meat-eater."

Together they stomped and swaggered past the sign, with the air of dinosaurs who owned the place. Before long, they spotted a pair of huge carnotaurs.

"Guards!" hissed Gipsy.

"Stop!" The biggest carnotaur lumbered over, his friend just behind him. "Who're you?"

Teggs gulped and tried not to lose his teeth. "Er . . . Us come from far away. Want to ride in rocket."

"You're nearly too late," snarled the second carnotaur. "What's the password?"

"Um . . . password?" Gipsy looked nervously at Teggs.

"All meat-eaters know the password. No password, no rocket-ride off the Earth." The biggest carnotaur loomed over them, his claws twitching. "And we will eat you alive for wasting our time. What is the password?" His drool-soaked jaws opened wider. "WHAT?"

Chapter Seven

CAMP OF FEAR

As the two carnotaurs hissed and growled, Teggs racked his brain for a possible password . . .

Suddenly Gipsy's bottom made a rude noise!

The biggest carnotaur stopped snarling, sniffed – and grinned. "Yep, that's the password all right!" He and his friend stood aside. "You can go."

"Phew!" Teggs grabbed the blushing Gipsy and hurried away up a hillside. "Nice work, Gipsy."

"Thank my bottom," Gipsy whispered. "I was so scared I couldn't control it — luckily for us."

Teggs nodded. "Let's hope our luck holds."

As the astrosaurs reached the crest of the hill, Teggs surveyed the carnivore camp. It was a far cry from the rusting, fume-filled, high-rise cities of his time. These primitive meat-eaters had set up a sprawling mess of grubby big-tops and tents and tepees stretching out for miles, all in the shadow of the line of chunky blood-red rockets.

Stealthily Teggs and Gipsy made their way down the slope and into the noisy, smelly heart of the camp. It was like a colossal carnivore carnival, with tribal drums booming and barbecues blazing.

"Trust this brutal bunch to be celebrating the end of the world," Gipsy muttered.

"I can't see Loki's death-flyer," said Teggs. "We'll have to search the whole area."

All breeds of meat-eater were crushed into the grotty tents, drinking swamp beer and fighting over food. The stench of dung and meat was everywhere. A T. rex came staggering out of a tent. "Roll up!" he rasped. "See Trixie the belly dancer! She'll be dancing with the chopped-off belly of a diplodocus!"

Teggs felt sick. "No, thanks."

"Have your future told by Madame Hagburger," leered a wrinkled oviraptor. He gestured to an old dinosaur in a filthy cloak with a cracked crystal ball, talking to a megalosaurus.

"I see you is going to be hit on the head," said Madame Hagburger – before socking her customer with a big stick.

As the megalosaurus groaned and fell over, Teggs and Gipsy jumped over his body and hurried on.

But suddenly there was a fanfare of trumpets close by and the loud music stopped abruptly. "Make way for the King!" came a growling shout. "Behold, King Rokol . . . and the Great Star Raptor!"

"Great Star Raptor?" Gipsy cringed. "That can only be—"

"Loki!" Teggs hissed as the crowds parted to reveal two dinosaurs sprawled on huge crimson sedan chairs, each carried by a pair of sweating T. rexes.

Loki lounged in one, resplendent in his black leather uniform, and in the other lay a vast maroon spinosaurus, a golden crown perched on his head and scarlet robes tight about his body. Slowly he rose to his taloned feet.

"Hear me, my subjects," King Rokol shouted. "It's the last night for Planet Earth. And our honoured guest, the Great Star Raptor, has shared with me a fiendishly flesh-licious plan."

"Indeed I have!" Now Loki rose from his seat. "As you know, I have already given you amazing weapons for your rockets that will allow you to conquer anyone you meet in space. How cool am I?"

"Very cool!" came the riotous response.

"Exactly!" Loki flung open his arms. "Now I say to you – why not test them out here on Earth – by using them against the plant-eater camp?"

Unhappy murmurings went up about the camp.

"Use machines to slay plant-scoffers instead of our teeth and claws?" cried a troodon. "That's not the meat-eater way."

King Rokol stood up with some difficulty. "The Star Raptor means that we can destroy their stupid electric fence with the new weapons."

Teggs and Gipsy swapped worried looks as the snarling, spitting crowd around them grew snarlier and spittier.

"That's right!" Loki yelled. "And while the plant-eaters panic, *we* shall attack. Why should those puny plant-eaters get away from the meteor when they can get in our stomachs?"

"Begin the bombardments!" boomed Rokol as the carnivores waved and cheered. "Once the way is clear, we shall catch and scrunch every last leaf-licker we can find!"

As Loki and the king were swept triumphantly away at the head of the braying meat-munching mob, Teggs put his communicator to his lips. "Arx, Iggy, can you hear me?"

"That won't work," Gipsy reminded him. "We're in the past, remember?"

"Of course." Teggs scowled. "Well, if we can't warn the plant-eaters, our only hope is to smash Loki's weapons before they smash the camp. Come on!"

He and Gipsy started pushing against the tide of carnivores rushing towards the exit.

"Get out of my way!" growled a huge allosaur.

"You get out of ours!" Teggs tried to barge past the brutal meat-eater, but there was a scuffle — and the chunks of mud hiding Teggs's backplates started crumbling away.

"Look out, Captain!" Gipsy couldn't help but shout — and as she did so, her false fangs fell out.

"Hey!" The big allosaur frowned at Teggs and Gipsy. "You're pretty funny-looking carnivores."

A young T.rex bundled up. "They not meat-eaters. They is *leaf-nibblers*!"

"We've been rumbled," squealed Gipsy.

"Plant-eaters!" someone bellowed. "Spies! Here in our camp!"

"Catch them!" came a blood-curdling cry. "*Eat* them!"

"Quick, Gipsy!" Teggs dragged her away and barged through the crowd of scowling, snarling meat-eaters all around them. His tail brushed against a huge flap of fabric – and he quickly tore it open. "Into this tent!"

Only once Teggs had ducked inside did he realize the dark and stinking tepee belonged to Madame Hagburger the fortune-teller. She was flossing her sharp teeth with a rusty hacksaw and scowled at her unexpected visitors.

"I'm having a tea break," she snapped. "Push off."

"But we're here to read *your* future," said Teggs quickly. "I see a big tail approaching your face at high speed . . ."

Madame Hagburger frowned – and Teggs conked her on the head.

"Hey," said the grizzled old dinosaur. "You're good!" Then she slid to the ground in a deep snooze.

"Hide her under the table," Teggs told Gipsy as he grabbed the fortune-teller's smelly cloak and wrapped it around himself. No sooner had Gipsy dragged Madame Hagburger under the tablecloth than a blood-red baryonyx burst inside with a rabble of other tough carnivores just behind him.

"Seen a couple of plant-eaters come in here?" he growled.

Teggs tried to impersonate the old fortune-teller and peered into the crystal ball. "Er . . . *yes*. I see them now . . . they are sneaking out of this camp. They are nearing the exit."

"We'll see about that," growled the baryonyx, as he turned and charged away. "Come on, you lot – let's go!"

Gipsy poked her head out from beneath the table. "Looks like meat-eaters were even stupider sixty-five million years in the past!"

"Lucky for us." Teggs got up. "Now, we must reach those carnivore rocket-ships – and make Loki's future weapons history!"

★

89

Back at the plant-eater camp, Iggy had taken a break from repairing Shuttle Alpha to check out the *Soar-a-saurus*'s whopping engines. The super-ship's power systems were an incredible lash-up, using random spare parts from dino-cars and trucks and cycles – but Iggy could find no reason why they wouldn't work. Once the six tug-ships had helped to tow the *Soar-a-saurus* into space, it would give thousands of plant-eaters the chance of a new life out among the stars.

"Hello, Mister." Zac's friend, Gazell the yellow stegosaurus, came into the power room, her hatchlings still squashed between her backplates. "How's it looking here? Find anything wrong?"

"No." Iggy smiled. "This ship should handle well, Gazell. I've checked the systems and they're all in working order. They just need a little oil."

"Aha." Gazell looked at her hatchlings. "Kids? Oil time!"

Iggy
blinked
as the
babies on
her back
produced oil-
cans from under
their blankets.
Holding them
with their tails,
they eagerly squirted
the ramshackle workings.

Gazell smiled to see Iggy
so astonished. "I'm from a whole family
of mechanics," she said. "Fixing engines
is in our blood!" Suddenly one naughty
hatchling started squirting *without* a can!
"Henri, that is not oil – don't be so dirty!"

Iggy smiled. "What are your nippers'
names?"

"Henri, Jim, Terry, Morris and . . ." She
frowned. "You know, I just can't decide
on a name for my youngest boy. It bugs

me day and night . . ." She sighed. "You
know, I think I'm just trying to distract
myself from how scary everything is
right now. I used to fix up broken buses
– now I'm supposed to fly the biggest
spaceship in history!"

"Have you had a chance to test-drive
the *Soar-a-saurus*?" Iggy wondered.

"Nope," Gazell admitted. "I'm just
gonna close my eyes, cross my legs and
hope I don't do what Henri just did!"
She shook her head. "We dinos should've
prepared for space travel a whole lot
sooner."

Iggy
remembered
what Arx
had said.
"Some
dinos went
to Venus
and Mars,
didn't they?"

"Sure, the Triassic beasts struck out into space," said Gazell. "And the sea-reptiles left to live on the moons of Jupiter a couple of centuries back, fed up with the carnivores trying to get them all the time . . . But I'm talking about *deep* space travel. We've already exhausted the solar system. And after the meteor hits, the Earth won't be back to normal for ages and ages. Zac says we've got to fly much further out, into the unknown . . . on a journey that'll last more than a million years . . ."

"And which will lead you into the Jurassic Quadrant," Iggy murmured. "Zac is right. It's what you have to do."

"Of course he's right," Gazell said. "He's brilliant! Since my husband was eaten by a gang of T. rexes last year, Zac has looked after me and my kids really well."

"I'm glad to hear it," said Iggy with a smile. "Good mechanics are hard to find!"

"So are test pilots." Arx came in, looking pleased. "Luckily, Zac is great! He and I have been testing the other five tug-ships. Once you've helped finish repairs to that one we hit, this amazing craft should be ready to fly!"

But suddenly a deep, muffled thunderclap shook through the *Soar-a-saurus*. Gazell jumped and her hatchlings nearly fell off her back. "What was that?" Another, louder explosion rocked the room, and metal tiles clattered from the walls and ceiling.

"Something's wrong," said Arx, charging from the room. "We'd better get outside. It sounds like we're under attack!"

Chapter Eight

CHAOS AT THE CAMP

When Iggy and Arx emerged with Gazell from the depths of the *Soar-a-saurus*, they found the sky alight with mega-bright streaks of ruby-red destruction – coming from the direction of the carnivore camp. Fires were breaking out all around. Distressed dinos were running round in a panic.

"Loki's firing his weapons," Iggy realized grimly.

KA-ZIZZ! The electric fence shook and sparked as red rays zapped against it. THTOOM! One whole section of the fence was blown apart . . . and the pieces smashed down on the cockpit of one of the tug-ships.

"No!" cried Gazell. "We can't lose our only way off this world . . . We *can't*!"

In the middle of the smoke and flames, a frantic Zac was directing the survival effort. "Pterosaurs, try to blow out the flames by flapping your wings really hard . . . You plateosaurus there, beat back the fires with blankets. Diplodocus, *stamp* out the flames – or try a well-aimed wee!"

Iggy, Arx and Gazell rushed up to help. When Zac saw Gazell he frowned. "It's not safe here. Take the children and find somewhere to hide."

Gazell shook her head. "I'll fetch the first-aid supplies and the doctors and nurses."

As she bravely ran off into the smoke with her hatchlings, Iggy and Arx watched the huge electric fence spit blue sparks high into the night and start to collapse completely.

"What are we going to do?" asked Iggy. "Loki's weapons are already taking out the fence.

They could
wreck the *Soar-
a-saurus* too—
OOF!"

A laser blast
nearby threw
Arx into Iggy,
knocking them both to the ground.
"We've got to reach Shuttle Alpha," said
Arx. "Quickly! It's our only chance."

"But the shuttle doesn't have any
weapons," Iggy protested. "What are we
going to do?"

"We're going to hope my wild plan
works out," said Arx grimly. "If it
doesn't, this entire place will go up in
smoke . . . and all our futures with it!"

Teggs carried Gipsy on his back as they
made their way towards the rockets. She
made sure to keep Madame Hagburger's
enormous cloak wrapped around them
both. Luckily – if you could call it that

– most carnivores had already fled their camp to get to the plant-eaters . . .

"I can't see a thing," Teggs complained through the smelly material. "Are we nearly there, Gipsy?"

"Yes." Gipsy could see the giant rockets towering ahead, their bolted-on weapons spitting laser bolts. "But there's no one firing the guns."

Teggs peeped out and saw a heavily armoured ship parked beside the red rockets. "There's Loki's death-flyer. Perhaps there's something inside we can use to destroy those weapons."

They hurried across to the death-flyer. The door was locked – but couldn't withstand a combined attack from the two angry astrosaurs. Once inside, Teggs scanned the controls. A black-and-yellow box had been wired messily into the main systems.

"That looks like a remote control unit," said Gipsy. Looking more closely, she saw that one button was labelled LASERS – and that it was switched on. "Hey! Loki must be controlling those weapons from here!"

"Makes sense," said Teggs. "Loki wouldn't want to hand over control of his weapons to Rokol, in case Rokol decided to get rid of him. So he's running the show from here." He fiddled with the black-and-yellow box. "But if we can just get those lasers to *reverse* their fire ..."

Gipsy grinned. "You mean, so they fire into themselves? That would make them go—"

100

BANG! One
after the other,
Loki's lasers blew
themselves apart,
scorching the
rockets they were
bolted to. Then
Teggs clobbered
the remote
control unit with
his tail – and it
exploded in white
smoke.

"You did it!" Gipsy
cried.

"But those lasers are bound to have
done some damage, and there are still
hundreds of carnivores racing towards the
plant-eater camp," said Teggs worriedly.
"How can we possibly stop them?"

Back at the plant-eater camp, Iggy was
running through the smoke-filled camp,

helping dinosaurs to safety – either getting them inside the *Soar-a-saurus* or hiding them behind the hunks of scrap metal lying around. No one in this time had ever seen a laser before or felt its effect. To them, such sheer power was terrifying – almost as terrifying as watching months of hard work being wrecked in minutes.

"Come on, Arx," Iggy muttered. "Your plan has just *got* to work!"

Then Iggy heard Zac's voice booming through the darkness. "It's not fair! Stop!" Suddenly he saw the stegosaurus, bellowing up at the smoky sky. "We were so close to escaping, so close to a new life. Stop raining fire on us! Stop!"

Iggy ran to him. "Er, Zac? I think the bombardment *has* stopped. Listen!"

An eerie hush had settled over the camp. There were no more zaps of energy, no more explosions. Timid plant-eaters began to poke their heads out from their makeshift shelters. Mothers and fathers comforted their frightened children.

"Thank goodness." Zac saw some large pterosaurs flap overhead. "Grab some torches and check out all the tug-ships and the *Soar-a-saurus*," he yelled. "Whatever's been damaged, we have less than a day to get it fixed."

Then a breathless pterodactyl swooped in to land beside them. "Carnivores sighted!" she squawked. "I spotted them from the air. Hundreds and hundreds of them – looking really fierce and headed this way!"

"But . . . the electric fence is all in bits." Zac groaned. "What can we do? First the carnivores softened us up. Now they're moving in for the kill!"

Iggy turned and shouted back the way he'd come. "Arx! Don't stop the work! The camp's got some uninvited dinner guests on the way – and we're the dinner!"

"What work?" said Zac. "What do you mean?"

But before Iggy could reply, the pterodactyl squawked at ear-splitting volume: "They're coming!"

Iggy and Zac peered through the haze of smoke and saw a seething sea of shadowy shapes surging down the hillside towards the camp. At their head were two elevated figures being carried on grand chairs.

"There's Loki,"

Iggy muttered. "There's nothing he loves more than a bit of destruction."

"And King Rokol too," said Zac. "So the meat-eaters win at last."

And then a small silver shape shot into sight over the dark haze of the hillside.

It was Loki's death-flyer!

Inside the stolen raptor ship, Gipsy peered out of the window while Teggs fought with unfamiliar controls to keep their flight steady.

"Carnivores right below us, Captain," called Gipsy. "They're almost at the camp. What are we going to do? We've blown up all Loki's weapons – now we've got none to use ourselves."

"We can use this whole *ship* as a weapon!" Teggs gave her a dangerous grin. "I'll take us in low . . ."

105

Gipsy gulped as the flyer dipped sharply and accelerated away — heading straight for King Rokol and Loki on their elevated sedan chairs. Both meat-scoffers turned in angry astonishment as Teggs gave a cheeky wave through the windscreen — then whooshed right over their heads. The enormous rush of wind as he passed by knocked both his targets out of their portable thrones. They landed with twin crunches on the ground below. "YEOWW-OOF!"

"Result!" Teggs cried.

"What about the rest of this rotten rabble?" asked Gipsy.

"Take the controls and I'll see what I

can do." As Gipsy gripped the flight stick, Teggs jumped up and crossed over to the flyer's cargo hold. "I think it's time those meat-heads learned what it's like to be bombarded from above!"

He opened the hold's outer doors. Then, bracing himself in the fierce gale, he curled his tail around a crate full of frozen meat and emptied it over the carnivores racing at the front of the pack. Some were struck and fell, others skidded to a stop and started chomping down the free food – only to be trampled and tripped over by the mass of meat-eaters behind.

"You might as well have the box, too!" Teggs yelled as he hurled the empty crate down at the crowd,

107

flattening a few more flesh-munchers. Then he hooked his tail spikes onto another crate, filled with electronic equipment. Hauling it over, he emptied the heavy machinery down on the ravenous dinos! Dozens were conked on the head and fell, flailing about in alarm.

But with a sinking heart, Teggs realized he couldn't hope to stop the sheer number of crazed carnivores racing towards Zac's camp.

"That meat-mad mob have almost reached the veggie camp!" Gipsy wailed. "The fence is in pieces – and any second now, the plant-eaters will be in pieces too!"

Chapter Nine

WALKING ON AIR

In the smoking fields of the plant-eater
camp, Iggy and Zac watched helplessly
as hordes of hate-filled carnivores
stormed through the gaps in
the electric fence.

Iggy was glad most
of the plant-eaters
were still sheltering
from the laser-
storm. That
wouldn't
save them
from the
invading
carnivores

– but at least they wouldn't know what was coming. "Right then, Zac!" he said gruffly. "If we're going down, let's go down fighting!"

Zac nodded and flexed his spiky tail, ready to rumble. The ravenous rabble of carnivores charged closer and closer . . .

And then – WHAMM!

It was as if they had slammed into an invisible wall. POMM! BAMM! PHOOM! Again and again the carnivores clonked into a barrier that Zac and Iggy couldn't see. More and more meat-eaters came piling in, squashing the ones who'd crashed into the solid air first – then crashing into it themselves.

Zac stared. "I don't get it. What's happened?"

"*Arx* happened!" cried Iggy as a weary but relieved-looking green triceratops ran towards them. "You did it, Arx. You managed to boost the shuttle's force field ..."

"Just about," Arx agreed. "I rewired the power systems and inflated the ship's energy shield until it covered the entire camp like a protective dome."

Zac gazed in wonder as the crushed-up carnivores bit and snapped at each other, struggling to get clear of the invisible barrier. Then he turned to Arx and bowed. "I don't know who you really are, or where you've come from, or *how* you've done it – but you've saved the camp!"

"And look up there!" Arx pointed

to Loki's death-flyer as it zoomed
overhead, with two familiar figures
waving through the windscreen. "It's
Gipsy and Captain Teggs!"

Iggy grinned. "I wondered
what that

raptor ship
was up to. The captain must've stolen it."

But suddenly the flyer spun round and
round, like a raptor chasing its tail.

"What are they doing?" Arx wondered.
"It's as if they've lost control . . ."

"I've lost control, Gipsy!" Teggs cried,
wrestling with the flyer's flight stick.
"This thing's not doing what I'm telling
it to do!"

"I think it's starting to do what *Loki* wants." Gipsy pointed out through the window. "Look!"

Teggs saw that Loki was back in his sedan chair, wielding a large silver handset. "It wasn't only the rocket weapons he designed to work by remote control. He's got power over this whole flyer – and he means to use it!"

"Of course," groaned Gipsy, helping Teggs grip the flight stick. "He couldn't take his raptors through time with him because he only stole one exo-suit – so he had an automatic pilot built in. Can we smash it like you smashed the weapons remote control?"

"It'll be built into the heart of the ship," said Teggs. "We'll never get to it in time." Suddenly the flight stick snapped off in his hand in a fizz of green sparks. "Uh-oh, that's torn it. Time to abandon ship!"

Gipsy's headcrest flushed electric blue. "We can't, we're too high up! We'll be squished!"

"There are still some crates left," shouted Teggs, stumbling dizzily to a couple of shiny boxes in the cargo area. "I think they're made of mega-metal. If we get inside one, it should cushion our fall!"

Gipsy scrambled into one of the crates, which was half full of electrical bric-a-brac. Teggs pushed it over to the open doorway, squeezed his upper body into the box next to Gipsy, and curled his tail against the floor like a giant spring. As the ship stopped spinning and began to move away under Loki's control, Teggs launched himself, Gipsy and the crate into empty space . . .

"Whoaaa!" Gipsy helped pull Teggs into the crate beside her. Neither of them knew where they were, or how high up, or how many carnivores were waiting to get them down below, or if the crate would even protect them from their crash landing ...

But after only a couple of seconds – POMM! The big metal box crunched against something solid.

"Ooof!" Teggs and Gipsy were thrown out of the crate like jack-in-the-boxes ...

And found themselves sprawled out in thin air, high above the plant-eater camp!

"Captain! Gipsy!" Arx yelled up at them. "You've landed on my force field!"

115

Teggs beamed down at his friends below. "Better than landing on our butts!"

Then a fierce and furious roar from King Rokol silenced the squashed and squabbling carnivores forced up against the force field.

"Newcomer from the stars," he hissed, rounding on Loki. "You promised us a wonderful night of battle, bloodshed and bone-chewing with your amazing weapons . . . but the plant-eaters have thwarted you and tricked us all. We haven't had so much as a nibble!"

"And you won't, either!" Teggs bellowed. "The star-raptor's weapons are weak compared to the powers of the . . . um . . ."

"The interplanetary plant-eaters!" said Gipsy quickly.

"Right!" Zac bellowed. "With our friends beside us, we're stronger than you meat-bloated bozos will ever be!"

"Curse you, astrosaurs!" Loki yelled.

"See how your mighty star-raptor fears us?" Arx joined in.

"Never forget, these veggie dinosaurs are well-defended." Teggs nodded at King Rokol. "And if you're not careful, we will attack YOU!"

"Nooo!" screeched an allosaurus, weeing himself in fright.

"They have supernatural powers!" a dryptosaurus sobbed. "They'll destroy us all!"

Rokol scowled at Loki. "What a rubbish end to our last day on Earth!" Angry growls of agreement went up from the carnivores all around. "We shall return to our own camp at once."

"Wait!" Loki had finally got full

control over his death-flyer, which hovered overhead like a giant metal hawk. "Please, your majesty. Ride with me in my, er, star chariot, so that I may share other plans with you."

"No!" Rokol declared. "Two of those interplanetary plant-eaters have been inside, and I bet they've left terrible traps. I shall be carried in my great throne as always. *You* can do what you like." With that – and a few barked commands at the chair bearers – he was taken on his teetering way, the carnivore crowds following in his wake.

Loki glared coldly at Teggs and Gipsy. "You haven't won yet. Just you wait!" And he brought his ship down low and scrambled inside.

Moments later the flyer soared away.

"I thought he'd never leave," said Teggs, watching as the other carnivores scuttled away over the hills and vanished into the night. "But now that he has – how are we going to get down from here?"

"You may not have to wait long, Captain," said Arx as the invisible shield began to wobble. "I had to boost the shuttle's force field to the limit, and any moment now it could go—"

POP! Suddenly Teggs and Gipsy were falling again. Iggy ran and caught Gipsy – while Teggs landed in a muddy puddle with a splash.

"Welcome back," said Arx happily.

"There's no time to waste on words." Teggs jumped up, shook himself dry and marched over to Zac. "We've only got tonight to put things right if you're going to leave before the meteor hits."

"It's no good," said Zac quietly. "I mean, thank you for all you've done to help us, but it's hopeless." He pointed up at a bright orange star in the sky. "Look, there's the meteor. It's going to destroy almost all life on the planet. And because I didn't protect this camp well enough, it's going to destroy us too."

"No way!"

Zac and the astrosaurs started at the loud, shrill voice. It belonged to Gazell, who was leading a long trail of fellow plant-eaters out of the battle-scarred *Soar-a-saurus*. Teggs could see nurse dinosurs with first-aid boxes, mechanics with tools clamped in their mouths, builders in hard-hats made from hollowed-out stone ... More and more plant-eaters came crowding out, dinosaurs who knew that it was their destiny to reach for the stars – or to die in the attempt.

"You've done so much for us, Zac," said Gazell. "You've looked after us, you've given us a way off this world and you've never let us down. We're not going to let *you* down now by allowing some dumb meteor to use us as target practice. We're going to work hard to fix this, and we're all going to work together." Her face softened as she smiled at Zac. "That is, if it's OK with you . . . Chief?"

Zac looked at Teggs. "But you and your friends are the ones who saved this camp. You should take charge – not me."

Teggs shook his head and lowered his voice. "These dinosaurs need a strong leader to help them through all the dangers and hardships of the voyage ahead. And believe me, they need *you* to be that leader." He spoke more loudly: "You're the one in charge, Zac. Tell us what to do, and we'll do it."

Zac gave him a grateful smile. "Well, Arx and Iggy are fantastic with machines. Could they lead a work party fixing the damage to the tug-ships, while you and Gipsy help Gazell organize repairs to the *Soar-a-saurus*? We'll need a full report on everything that's been damaged. Oh, and we should take a register, too, to make sure no one is missing."

"We'll work all night," Gazell promised, and her hatchlings nodded too. "Won't we, everyone?"

Cries of eager agreement rose up into the night.

If all goes well, thought Teggs, *this will be the final night of dinosaurs on the Earth. But if it doesn't . . .*

He shivered as Loki's last words echoed in his head: *You haven't won yet. Just you wait!*

Chapter Ten

AN UNEXPECTED GIFT

The orange pinprick of the approaching meteor burned in the dark sky like an omen of doom. Even as dawn broke over the plant-eater camp, it lingered high overhead.

Not a single plant-eater was idle down on the Earth. With just six hours to go before impact, there was still too much to do.

Teggs yawned and stretched, then got back to hammering rivets into the side of the newly-repaired *Soar-a-saurus*. A ragbag

team of dino-teens
and old timers
were pushing
them into
place for Teggs
to clobber with
his tail.

He looked
around. Iggy
and Arx were just overseeing the final
work on the tug-ships. Gazell and some
friends were loading the last crates of
food and supplies on board. A gaggle of
triceratops students – their horns dipped
in ink and with large slates to write on –
had been visiting the thousands of cabins
on board the enormous ship, making sure
that all the passengers were safely inside
and ready to go; now Gipsy was checking
their findings.

Zac bustled up to Teggs, looking
absolutely whacked. "How are we doing
here?"

125

Teggs walloped the last of the rivets. "Finished!"

"And not a moment too soon," said Zac. "Well done, you guys."

Gipsy came along. "Well, Zac, we've counted five hundred thousand, eight hundred and ninety-nine dinos on board. The rest are all out here finishing work. All the eggs are on board, and the dino-gym is fully equipped so that everyone can keep fit on the voyage."

"Thanks, Gipsy," said Zac. "I'm beginning to think we might just get off this planet in time after all."

"But we have trouble, Zac," said Gazell, and the hatchlings on her back wriggled around. "The farmers have been checking the harvest. Those awful red lights last night set fire to half our food supplies. We'll have starved before we reach the nearest star!"

"Can't you grow plants on board the *Soar-a-saurus*?" asked Teggs.

"Yes, but there are thousands to feed, and the plants will take time to grow," Zac explained.

"Perhaps you can stock up again at a nice planet along the way," said Gipsy.

Zac shook his head. "There isn't one. The worlds of the solar system are not as abundant as the Earth. The reptiles in local space can barely feed themselves — we were planning to collect them on our way out."

Gazell pointed past them. "Well, right now we've got a worse problem. Look!"

Zac groaned, and the astrosaurs stared in dismay at the sight of a familiar figure in a sedan chair appearing over the hilltop once again.

"King Rokol and his carnivores," Gipsy whispered. "They're back!"

"What do they want now?" Teggs saw that Loki was not with Rokol this time – and nor was his wild rabble of followers. Instead, a procession of twenty-four hefty meat-stuffers of various breeds came alongside Rokol, each carrying five huge baskets. And in the baskets were . . .

"Plants?" Teggs stared in astonishment. "Are those meat-eaters bringing *plants*?"

Alerted by the cries, Arx and Iggy came charging over from the tug-ships to join Teggs and Gipsy.

"What is Rokol playing at?" wondered Iggy.

"Get everyone inside, Gazell," said Zac firmly. "I'll see what the carnivores want this time."

While Gazell got busy, Zac and the astrosaurs walked over to meet the sharp-toothed king.

"Hear me, plant-eaters – you have nothing to fear!" called Rokol. "I come with gifts for you all."

"Gifts?" Teggs looked suspicious.

"It's true," Rokol insisted, gesturing to his slaves to set him down a safe distance away from the camp's broken fence. "I should

never have listened to that fool Loki
from the stars. But last night . . . well,
you know how it is. We'd finished our
packing, we had cool new weapons to
try out, we had a few cups of swamp
beer too many and got a bit carried
away trying to squish you and blow you
all up. But the thing is – we're sorry."

Zac raised his eyebrows. "Really?"

"Really!" Rokol bowed his head.
"When you and your interplanetary
plant-eaters demonstrated your strength
and special powers . . . I was impressed,
and so were my people."

Rokol's slaves nodded, staring at Teggs
and Gipsy. "You walked on the air!" said
one.

"You built invisible walls," said another,
looking at Arx and Iggy.

"And you destroyed the magic weapons
of the weakling star raptor." Rokol
shuddered. "I do not wish to see these
powers used against us – especially since

we can't hurt
you back with
our rocket lasers
destroyed. So!
As a peace
offering, we
would like you
to accept these."

The king
snapped his
claws and his
subjects came forward
to place the baskets of
potted plants in front of Zac.

"These . . . these are garga-weeds!" Zac
stared in amazement. "The more you eat,
the faster they grow – which is why the
carnivores destroyed most of them."

"Of course," boomed Rokol. "There
are quite enough plant-eaters about
already—" He broke off and forced a
chuckle. "But we have learned the error
of our ways. And so, now we give them

to you freely – as long as you promise to leave us alone."

"We'll see about that," said Iggy. "It could be a trick."

"This gift might be poisoned!" Gipsy agreed.

"Let me examine them," said Arx. "I'm a bit of an expert on plants."

"And I'm an expert at eating them!" said Teggs, his tum rumbling.

The carnivores cringed as Teggs and Arx approached, and pushed forward their baskets.

Arx picked out one of the thick, sticky plants and sniffed its yellow flowers. Then he turned to Teggs and lowered his voice. "I read that garga- weeds grew here on old Earth but were lost on the great journey into space."

Teggs couldn't resist – he nibbled a leaf – and sure enough, another grew to replace it. "Mmmm!" The garga-weed tasted super-delicious. "It doesn't *seem* to be poisoned." He tried another leaf from another plant in another basket. And another. And another! "Mmm, lovely . . ."

Gipsy grinned. "Save some for Zac, Captain!"

Zac looked up at King Rokol. "Thank you for this kind gift. We shall, er . . . let you leave Earth."

"Phew!" Rokol smiled again as his servants put down their baskets. "I am glad we will know a new age of peace – at least while we journey out through space." He signalled to his slaves, who lifted him in his chair and carried him off. "Farewell!"

Rokol's band followed on behind without a backward glance. Soon, all of them were out of sight.

Zac chewed on a garga-weed, and marvelled as its leaves grew straight back again. "Rokol has given us the perfect gift. Now we won't starve after all!"

Arx beamed. "I'll run a couple of tests on these to make sure they're definitely all right . . ."

"And then we must help your passengers get ready for lift-off in the *Soar-a-saurus*," said Teggs excitedly. "There's not much time left, but they'll make it after all – together with a never-ending lunch!"

Within half an hour, Arx had tested leaves from each enormous basket and declared them all safe. Gazell wasted no time in organizing a work party to heave the haul on board. Then the astrosaurs joined Zac in the control room of the biggest tug-ship.

It was like a huge cube split into three levels. The controls were massive, built mainly into the floor so that the dinosaurs could work them with their clumsy feet. A large pterosaur was perched beside an enormous steering wheel, ready to work it with her beak.

"This is like standing inside an antique," Iggy murmured, gazing around. "Fantastic!"

"Once the tug-ships have pulled the *Soar-a-saurus* out into space, Gazell will take full control," Zac explained. "The tug-ships will then join onto the *Soar-a-saurus* and their energy probes will help power her systems. We can also use them as our shuttle craft for visiting new worlds."

"It's going to be an incredible adventure," said Teggs, ushering his crew towards the exit ladder. "I wish we could share it with you."

Zac looked puzzled as they started climbing down the rungs. "But you'll come with us, won't you?"

"We'll, er, follow you into space in our own ship," Teggs said. "You see, there's somewhere in particular we have to get to . . ."

"A long, long way from here," said Gipsy.

"Well, good luck." Zac shook hands and feet with all the astrosaurs as he followed them outside. He took a last look around at the scorched valley and the mountains as a clutch of colossal, clunky rocket-ships tore across the sky like deep red scratches in the blue.

"There goes Rokol and his carnivores," said Iggy. The rockets soon faded from sight. But the orange dot of the meteor burned ever more brightly.

"Time we were gone." Zac looked round at the other enormous tug-ships, two on either side of his own. He held up a big green flag to them, and the pilots waved green flags back at him. "With just an hour to spare, we're ready to go . . ." He climbed back up the ladder and waved to the astrosaurs. "So long!"

"So long *ago*," breathed Teggs as Zac got back into his tug-ship's control room. "And yet here we are, ready for—"

"BLAST OFF!" Zac hollered, and his tug-ship's engines fired into life with an incredible roar. The astrosaurs clung together as the ground began to shake. The four remaining tug-ships started up their mighty motors. Finally the *Soar-a-saurus*'s engines ignited with a rumbling thunderclap that seemed loud enough to shatter mountains.

Awestruck, Teggs watched the fierce blue flames gusting from the tug-ships' several jets, as each of them took

138

to the air. Their towropes, tied to the sides of the *Soar-a-saurus*, grew taut and tightened as they strained to help lift the ark-ship's titanic weight. Teggs whooped with delight as the *Soar-a-saurus*'s engines roared even louder and thick, dungy exhaust smoke swirled all around, while the giant jets' flames turned incandescent white. Then, finally, the humongous craft rose into the sky, the tug-ships taking her higher and higher . . .

"Have a good trip!" Gipsy hooted at top volume, and Iggy waved as the unlikely spaceships slowly dwindled from view into the upper atmosphere.

"That was amazing," said Teggs. "To think we saw such a historic moment with our own eyes."

Arx nodded, eyeing the meteor in the

sky. "But now it's time we were gone too."

"How true!" came a horrid hiss from behind them.

With a sinking feeling, Teggs turned to find that a familiar black-and-orange figure with an eye-patch had sneaked up in the storm of noise, smoke and dirt.

It was General Loki, a glint of evil relish in his only eye – and an atom gun clutched in his claws!

Chapter Eleven

A TRICK IN TIME

"You thought you could thwart my plans, didn't you?" rasped Loki. "Well, you were wrong!"

"We *have* thwarted them." Teggs squared up to the black-clad raptor.

"You might just have noticed the *Soar-a-saurus* has taken off – with thousands of plant-eaters safely aboard."

Loki chuckled. "Aboard perhaps, but not safely."

"What do you mean?" asked Arx.

"You checked those plants for poison," said Loki. "But you should have tested the *soil* in which they grew. Then you might've found the twelve bombs I'd hidden inside random pots!"

Gipsy and Iggy gasped, and Teggs stared in horror. "Bombs?"

"Magnificent micro-bombs!" Loki nodded gloatingly. "Super-explosive gunpowder sealed in a mega-metal shell. Completely tamper-proof! Once set, they cannot be defused."

Teggs scowled. "So Rokol *was* tricking us."

"No! The soft fool really did wish to suck up to you sap-sucking stinkheads." Loki spat on the ground. "He threw me

out of his camp —
I had to sneak
back inside
and plant
my bombs in
those baskets
when no one
was looking!"

"How long
before the explosives
go off?" Iggy demanded.

"They are set to detonate just
as the meteor strikes the Earth." Loki
sniggered. "The puny plant-eaters will
perish at the same time as their planet!"

Gipsy looked pale. "Captain, that
awful future we found at the other end
of the space tunnel, where meat-guzzling
dinos ruled the Earth and Mars and
everywhere else, and plant-eaters don't
exist . . . It's all going to happen, isn't it?"

"You've *seen* this future?" Loki's eyes
widened, and he cackled with delight.

"There you are, then – proof, astrosaurs, of your ultimate defeat!"

"No," said Teggs. "That was how the future was *before* we travelled back here to stop you. Now we're a part of history ourselves, we can put events back on track."

Loki waved his gun. "While I've got this? I don't think so."

"You haven't used it yet," Teggs observed coolly. "Which means you must want something from us."

"Correct." Loki narrowed his single eye. "When you stole my ship you threw out three mega-metal crates. One of those crates contained food, one contained spare parts for my death-flyer . . . and the last contained my exo-suit."

Teggs's eyes widened. "And without that, you can't escape in your stolen time machine, can you?"

"But I must!" cried Loki. "First I shall make sure Rokol and his fleeing carnivores know it was I who killed all the plant-eaters, so that I'll become a legend throughout the universe. Then, when I return to my own time, I shall be a dinosaur god, worshipped by all! I'll have power over everyone and everything! So – hand over my exo-suit at once."

"But . . . we don't have it!" Gipsy protested.

Teggs nodded. "We used that crate to cushion our fall – but we didn't see your exo-suit inside."

"Captain!" Iggy gasped. "I've just realized – Zac told his helpers to gather up all the spare parts they could find in case they were useful in the future."

"But these parts are *from* the future," said Arx. "If dinosaurs today discover the secrets of technology that won't be invented until sixty-five million years from now . . ."

"It could change history as surely as those bombs will," said Teggs gravely. "We've got to get up to the *Soar-a-saurus* and sort things out!"

"Bah. So sickeningly noble as ever." Loki raised his gun. "All I care about is getting hold of an exo-suit. Give me yours, Teggs – or I'll shoot your friends."

"All right . . ." said Teggs slowly. "I'll fetch it."

"No tricks," Loki warned. "Or the stripy girl gets it first!"

Gipsy, Arx and Iggy watched helplessly as Teggs trudged over to the *Sauropod's* shuttle, went inside and shut the door. Loki chuckled nastily.

"What are you laughing at?" came a familiar voice behind them.

Everyone spun round . . . to find Teggs was somehow behind them, and wearing his exo-suit! He punched Loki in the snout, and the raptor general went down like a sack of potatoes.

"Captain!" squealed Gipsy in delight.

Iggy was baffled. "But we saw you get on board the shuttle. How can you be in two places at once?"

"The same way he could be in two places at once back at the space prison," said Arx, smiling. "When he went to the shuttle he must've put on his exo-suit and used the time machine to send himself five minutes back into the past!"

"Exactly!" Teggs agreed.

"But the pyramid blew a fuse when it brought us here," Gipsy remembered.

"I tried pressing the blue demonstration button as Zindi did," Teggs told her. "There must have been just enough power left to send myself back to when the *Soar-a-saurus* was taking off. While

149

we were busy watching it and Loki was creeping up . . ."

"*You* crept up behind us all!" Gipsy realized.

"And I've been hiding behind that rock ever since," Teggs revealed, "just waiting to make a surprise reappearance and come to our rescue!"

Arx looked forlorn. "If only I'd fixed the time machine right away, we could travel back to this morning when Loki was planting his bombs and stop him!"

"Can't you do it now?" Iggy asked him.

"It might take hours and hours." Arx shook his head. "Always assuming I can do it at all!"

"Then we'll have to do things the hard way," Teggs said gravely. "Come on, let's drag Loki onto our shuttle and get after the *Soar-a-saurus*. The meteor's going to hit within the hour."

"And when it does," said Arx, "those bombs on board will explode. If we can't find them and defuse them in time, the plant-eaters will die, and Loki's twisted future will become reality."

Teggs nodded. "That's why we've got to succeed – we've just *got* to!"

Minutes later the astrosaurs were taking off in Shuttle Alpha. Loki lay sprawled in a heap at Teggs's feet, and did not stir as the small ship blasted away from the planet in a whirlwind of fire and dung-flavoured smoke.

"Step on it, Iggy," Teggs urged his friend as the shuttle soared up and away and the sky turned to space around them.

"If only communicators existed in this time!" Gipsy lamented. "We've got no way to warn Gazell and Zac of the danger they're in."

"Look! There's the *Soar-a-saurus*, up ahead." Arx pointed through the windscreen to where the enormous ramshackle ship was speeding through space; the tug-ships had done their job and were now fixed to its sprawling sides just as Zac had described. "And there's the meteor!"

Teggs swallowed hard. The meteor was close enough now to be clearly visible – a jagged rock miles across, tumbling out of the void on its deadly collision course with the Earth. "Head straight for the *Soar-a-saurus*, Ig."

"But there's nowhere to dock!" Iggy protested. "We can't get on board."

Teggs was already changing into his spacesuit. "I'll just have to spacewalk across to the cargo hold and use Loki's gun to blow a hole in the door. Everything's strapped down in there, so it shouldn't fall out into space."

"You can use this sealing foam to block up the hole once you're inside." Gipsy passed Teggs a heavy spray can and he pushed it into his pocket. "Just like Iggy blocked the hole that Zac's tug-ship made in this shuttle."

"And since Loki hid the bombs in those baskets, he'll be the best one to find them." Teggs hauled the unconscious Loki to his feet and started stuffing him into another spacesuit. "Once he knows he'll be blown up along with his victims when the meteor hits Earth, I think he'll be willing to help."

Iggy steered alongside the *Soar-a-saurus*. Keeping tight hold of the general, Teggs took a long white rope that was attached to a metal platform at the back of the shuttle and clipped it to his suit. "Space ejector ready?"

"Ready," Iggy confirmed.

Teggs stood on the platform with Loki and took a deep breath. He had reached the final, desperate stage of the most vital mission of his life . . .

"Send me out there, Ig," Teggs said. "Now!"

Chapter Twelve

DISASTER IN SPACE

Teggs gasped as the space ejector platform
shot upwards on a big pole. At the same
moment, a hatch in the ceiling slid open,
and he and Loki were pushed out into
starry darkness. The platform filled the
hatch-space so perfectly that not a breath
of air escaped from the shuttle. Teggs felt
a thrill of fear – had it not been for the
rope tethering his space suit to the shuttle

roof, he and Loki would be left drifting helplessly through the cosmos.

And the plant-eater population would perish with us, he thought.

Like a determined diver, Teggs used the shuttle roof as a springboard and launched himself towards the *Soar-a-saurus*'s cargo hold. He held Loki's wrist in one hand and the atom gun in the other.

But suddenly the tricky raptor twisted in his grip – and snatched the gun away!

Loki was only pretending *to be asleep*, Teggs realized. He tried to grab back the gun, but Loki kicked him in the belly and sent him crashing into the side of the *Soar-a-saurus*. Then, with an evil grin, the raptor put his gun to the space-rope and fired right through it.

Teggs's worst nightmare had come
true – he was floating helplessly in space!
Desperately he scrabbled for a grip on
the giant ship, and just caught hold of
one of the cargo door handles. Clinging
on, he saw Loki's drooling jaws twist
wide in a grin as he prepared to fire . . .

Back on the shuttle, Arx, Iggy and
Gipsy watched the drama unfold in
horror.

"Poor Teggs!" cried Gipsy. "He's done
for!"

But then, with his free hand, Teggs grabbed the sealant spray and fired it at Loki's space helmet – SPLAT! Thick white foam covered the raptor's faceplate, and left him blinded.

Gipsy, Arx and Iggy cheered – but then Loki started firing wildly. One blast almost hit Teggs in the leg, another narrowly missed his back.

"Hang on, you two." Iggy twisted hard on the shuttle's flight stick. "I'm going to spoil Loki's aim!"

Gipsy and Arx gasped as their ship began to roll in a dizzying spin.

Dangling from the rope
like a conker on the end
of a string, Loki was
swung round and round
the shuttle. But still he
was firing wildly.

"Nice job, Ig," said Gipsy
as an atom-blast zipped
past the windscreen. "But if
he hits us, we haven't got any
more sealing foam to keep in the air!"

Iggy groaned. "How can we get the
captain back inside?"

Arx watched as the massive meteor
rolled ever nearer. "And how can we get
Loki's bombs out of the *Soar-a-saurus*?"

"If only there was more metal on the
captain's spacesuit," said Gipsy, "we could
use our space magnets to pull him back!"

Iggy shook his head. "We'd pull the
Soar-a-saurus towards us too. It would
crash into the shuttle . . ."

Suddenly Arx jumped into the air.

"Maybe not!" he cried, turning to the main controls and jabbing them with his horns. "If I can only change the settings in time ..."

Gipsy stared. "What do you mean? What are you doing?"

"Trying to solve all our problems at once!" Arx yanked a wire from one circuit and plugged it into another. "Keep everything crossed, you two. We're going to need all the luck we can get!"

ZZAP! Dodging another of Loki's laser beams, Teggs banged with all his strength on the cargo hold's door. If only someone would let him inside – before it was too late. Already he could feel his grip on the

handle begin to slip. If he
let go now, he'd be lost
in space for ever . . .

Suddenly
something smashed
against the doors of
the cargo hold – from the
inside. CLANG! CLANG!! *CLANG!!!*
A series of little impacts sent vibrations
through the metal. And behind Loki,
Shuttle Alpha was starting to shake.
Teggs saw that its space magnets were
fully extended and shining an eerie blue.
He frowned. *Normally they glow red. What's
going on?*

Then the cargo doors were smashed
wide open by one of Loki's crates,
which had come whizzing
out from
inside.

Teggs clung to the handle as a dozen gleaming metal spheres swiftly followed it out into space like big bullets in a cloud of frozen soil.

"The bombs!" he breathed. "Somehow they've been sucked out of the *Soar-a-saurus*!"

Hope swelled inside Teggs's chest and gave him new strength to hold on. He watched in amazement as the shuttle switched off its magnets and shot upwards to avoid the deadly shower of bombs. Loki too was jerked up in the air like a puppet on a string as the projectiles hurtled past. Then the shuttle dropped back down again into position alongside the *Soar-a-saurus* and its magnets switched on again, shaking with power.

"Of course!" Teggs cried, his heart pounding. "Arx must've changed the magnets' settings so they only attract *mega*-metal!"

Still holding onto the space-rope, Loki finally clawed the foam from his helmet. "Curse you, astrosaurs!" he screamed, his one eye bright and narrowed with rage. "Curse you all, throughout eternity!"

"If I were you, Loki, I'd spend less time cursing and more time getting ready to dodge," Teggs cried. "If I'm right about our magnets attracting mega-metal — and if I've counted correctly — there are still two crates packed away on board the *Soar-a-saurus*. Any minute now you should be able to see for yourself . . ."

Right on cue, both big metal crates
came rocketing out from inside the cargo
hold. Loki had time for just a single
squawk of outrage – then dropped both
his gun and the rope as the biggest crate
slammed into him. Again, Shuttle Alpha
turned off its magnets and steered aside
before Loki and his cube of mega-metal
could crash into it. Instead, the crate's
momentum carried
the evil raptor
out through
space . . .

And straight into the path of the oncoming meteor!

SPLAMMMM! Teggs winced, his insides twisting in shock as the colossal rock roared past, snatching Loki, the crate and everything inside it from sight.

"Pulverized," Teggs muttered in shock. "My oldest enemy . . . gone for ever."

It was a terrible end to a terrible life, he decided.

But somehow, it seemed a fitting one.

Chapter Thirteen

GETTING BACK

Teggs was still dangling helplessly when
two big, quilted, spiky somethings dropped
down in front of his face.

They were
stegosaurus tails –
in spacesuits!

Gratefully, Teggs
let go of the cargo
door handle and
held onto the tails
as Zac and Gazell
heaved him inside.
Amid scattered
plants and baskets, Teggs
could see them both – and Gazell's little

hatchlings – all wearing space helmets and looking down at him with concern.

"Teggs!" said Zac. "I thought you weren't coming with us?"

"We heard all the banging," said Gazell. "What's been going on? It looks like a bomb went off in here!"

Teggs gave her a crooked smile. "You're closer than you know." He pointed to where the Earth's disc was slowly dwindling in the distance. "What's about to happen there will tell us if we're safe or—"

Even as he spoke, a pinprick of light flared on the surface of the planet: the nameless meteor had struck. Teggs watched, transfixed, as a dark cloud billowed up from the fiery spot and began to blanket the Earth.

"The end," he murmured. "And a new beginning."

Then twelve fierce explosions bloomed in nearby space as Loki's bombs went off – harmlessly. The hatchlings oohed and ahhed at the storm of fire and light, staring in wonder.

"Whoa!" Zac shielded his eyes. "What was that?"

"That," said Teggs, "was the end of poor old loopy Loki's final evil scheme to wipe you out. Thanks to my amazing crew, it failed."

Zac blinked, bewildered. Then he grinned and shook Teggs by the hand. "You four have done so much to help us. We shall sing your praises every day, all across space, so you will never be forgotten."

"Er, actually –" Teggs smiled ruefully – "it's probably a good idea if you keep very, very quiet about us. I can't explain, but it's for the best."

"Well," said Gazell, "there's one thing I can do to remember you." She scooped her youngest hatchling from her back and held him up to Teggs. "I've finally decided what to call this little tyke! I shall name him after *you*."

"Wow! Cool!" Teggs blushed. "So he'll be Teggs, er ... I'm sorry, Gazell, I don't know your second name ..."

"I'd like it to be 'Stegosaur'," Zac blurted. "Gazell – will you marry me?"

Gazell stared at him in shock. Then she hugged him tight and her hatchling jumped on him too. "Yes! Yes, I will!"

Teggs gulped. *So there he is*, he thought. *Teggs Stegosaur the first!*

Could it be possible? Was he looking at his own distant ancestor – his great-great-great-times-a-million-billion-great-grandfather?

A little dizzily, Teggs turned to the *Sauropod* shuttle flying alongside, and saw Iggy, Arx and Gipsy waving through the windows. He saluted them, and then waved back happily.

It's hard to know for sure, Teggs decided. *But right now, I think the future for us all is looking very bright indeed!*

A few minutes later, with super-precise steering, Iggy brought Shuttle Alpha right alongside the *Soar-a-saurus* so that Teggs could simply hop from the cargo hold onto the little ship's roof! He landed on the hatch cover, grabbed hold of the remains of the rope, and took a final look back at the distant, raging Earth.

Then the ejector platform sucked him back inside – and into the waiting arms of his happy friends.

"Captain!" Arx cried. "Thank space you're back safely."

Teggs grinned. "Thank space *you* rejigged the magnets to work only on mega-metal."

Arx looked pleased. "Oh, it was nothing really."

"I don't think Loki would thank you," Iggy declared. "So it's just as well there's nothing really left of him – or his death-flyer, that time machine or any other technology, now that the meteor's trashed it all."

"But will there be anything left of our future?" said Gipsy nervously. "Has our being here in the past helped history stay on track – or wrecked it?"

"If Arx can only fix the time machine, we'll find out," said Teggs, already stripping off his quilted space gear. "By travelling forward sixty-five million, one hundred thousand and fifty-six years to the present – where this all began!"

Teggs thought he might go crazy, cooped up in the little shuttle for hours and hours, wondering if they would be trapped in the past for ever. But although it took Arx the better part of a day, he was able to repair the golden pyramid in the end. The astrosaurs put on their exo-suits and prepared for the first leg of their long journey back home.

Arx nudged the time machine's on-button with his nose-horn. "Here goes everything," he murmured as the metal pyramid hummed into life.

At once, Teggs felt the shuttle begin to shudder and shake. The familiar flash of red light sparked through his head. He was spinning, spiralling, lost . . .

Then, with a gigantic lurch, the shuttle stopped shaking and all was still. Teggs let out a sigh of relief and opened his eyes.

"I think we're back in our own time, Captain," Arx said breathlessly, studying the time machine's readout.

Iggy checked the shuttle controls. "We're back where we started, between Earth and Mars."

"It all seems quiet," said Gipsy, staring out into space. "But did we win, or . . . ?"

She left the question hanging.

"*Sauropod*," said Teggs, speaking urgently into the communicator. "This is your captain in Shuttle Alpha. Can you hear me?"

Only whispers of static could be heard through the speakers.

Teggs tried again. "Come in, *Sauropod*, please?" He swallowed hard. "Anyone?"

Then a loud chirp came through loud and clear.

Gipsy cheered. "It's Sprite!"

A babble of chirps crackled from the communicator, and Gipsy quickly translated for Iggy's benefit: "*Captain, I don't know what happened. One minute those crazy carnivore ships were shooting us with everything they had, the next they—*"

"Vanished?" Teggs interrupted.

Sprite made squawks and clicking noises. "*Yes!*" Gipsy continued. "*The bad carnivores just faded away. It was as if . . . they'd never existed.*"

"That's because they never *did* exist."

177

Arx was grinning as he stared through his astro-scope. "Look at the Earth! Just look at it!"

Teggs, Iggy and Gipsy quickly crowded round to see. There were no giant snarling reptiles all over the place. The planet was plastered with billions of human beings.

Gipsy whooped. "The Earth's back to normal!"

"If you can call those funny-looking humans normal!" said Iggy.

"Right now, I call them the most welcome sight in the universe," said Teggs. "All this proves that we haven't harmed history after all – we've simply given it a helping hand. So let's catch up with the *Sauropod* and travel back through the space tunnel. I'm glad we visited Earth, but now I'm ready to stay in the real home of the dinosaurs."

"The Jurassic Quadrant," said Gipsy dreamily. "I can't wait!"

Chapter Fourteen

PRESENT IN THE PRESENT!

Although shaken and battered – much like her crew – the *Sauropod* held together stoutly on the bone-jarring, mind-squashing return voyage through the space tunnel. And when the astrosaurs arrived at DSS HQ, they were informed that Admiral Rosso was waiting for them in the cavernously grand Extra-Special Suite for Very Important Dinosaurs.

As Teggs led his tired, terrific team through the suite's marble doors, he saw that Rosso wasn't alone. A whole crowd of dinos were gathered there with party poppers.

"SURPRISE!" came the huge shout

from all assembled, as the poppers went off and streamers flew. The dimorphodon launched joyfully into the air, catching the streamers and twirling them about like banners.

"You and your crew have done the plant-eater race proud this day, Teggs," Rosso declared. "And so I thought you deserved a small reward – the biggest, poshest party in dinosaur history!"

Iggy grinned. "We know a lot about history, sir!"

"So, party on, dudes!" A stocky green diplodocus stepped out from behind the admiral, with a yellow pterosaur perched on his back.

"Dutch! Blink!" Teggs beamed as his old team-mates from Astrosaurs Academy rushed forward to greet him. "It's so good to see you!"

"And you!" Blink squawked happily.

182

"And wherever the Daring Dinos go, can Damona's Darlings be far away?" A pretty red diceratops stepped forward to join them. "Hi, everyone!"

"Damona!" Teggs cried. "My old Academy rival, how are you?"

"Brilliant, of course!" Damona fluttered her eyelids. "As are *my* old team-mates, Splatt and Netta . . ."

"Wow," said Teggs as Netta the pink ankylosaur gave him a hug and Splatt the dryosaurus shook his hand. "The old gang really is all here."

"Along with some newer faces too," said Governor Bunwinkle, their friend from the space prison. "Well done, astrosaurs."

"Yes, and thank you," said Zindi Bent beside him, free of chains now. "Thank you for stopping Loki using my machine to destroy history."

Rosso smiled down at her. "Zindi is being released at once with a full pardon," he revealed. "She will join our top inventors' team at Super-Secure-Space-Station One, using her amazing mind to build many more marvellous machines that will help sea-reptiles and plant-eaters alike."

"I'm pleased to hear it," said Teggs.

Zindi grinned. "Well, you've certainly proved to me that my time machine is way too dangerous to stay in existence."

"Indeed it is," Rosso agreed. "Tomorrow, we'll take it to pieces. But right now, all of you

– enjoy the party! I've laid on the biggest buffet in the galaxy . . ."

"Laid on it? I hope you didn't squash it, dude," joked Dutch.

"Eeep," agreed Sprite as two dozen dimorphodon fell about with laughter.

"It's the way he tells them," said Netta dryly.

But Teggs hardly heard them. His eyes were out on stalks at the sight of the super-big table at the back of the room, weighed down with about a thousand plates of succulent-looking plants – including one that looked very familiar. "That's never a bowl of garga-weeds is it?"

"Newly discovered by the Supply Fleet on a distant planet," said Splatt proudly.

"That's a blast from the past I'm happy to see!"

Hunger and happiness filling his whole body, Teggs ran over and started tucking in greedily. "Delicious!"

Arx, Iggy and Gipsy ran over to join him in filling their plates.

"It's hard to believe that Zac and Gazell lived so many millions of years ago," said Gipsy. "I wish we could visit them a few years later to see how they got on . . ."

"Too dangerous," Arx declared.

"I'm sure they took good care of each other," said Iggy. "And of their family."

Including the very first little Teggs Stegosaur,
thought Teggs happily.

He looked around the room again
and saw other old friends in the crowd.
There was Shazz, the High Flapper
from Squawk Major, talking to Sprite
and the dimorphodon . . . Prime
Rhino Serras from the sunny world of
Hawn was chatting to Jodril, the big-
eyed apatosaurus . . . Queen Soapi the
bactrosaur was fanning herself weakly
while Leefer, the astrosaurs' smelly farmer

friend from Noxia-4, told her tales about his life . . . Spink, a friendly kentrosaurus miner, was chatting with Hank and Crank, star athletes of the Great Dinosaur Games . . .

Teggs wandered around the room, talking and laughing with them all for hours. He was glad to see his crew having fun too. Arx was delighted when his niece Abbiz burst in and came rushing up to hug him, just as Iggy was thrilled to find his brother Wimvis on the scene with two frothing flagons of top-quality fern-juice.

Gipsy broke off from a chinwag with Netta and Damona and tapped Teggs on the shoulder. "You looked miles away, Captain. A penny for your thoughts?"

"I was just thinking – who needs a time machine?" said Teggs. "With good friends and memories, we can relive past escapades whenever we like – and look forward to new adventures still to come."

"I'll drink to that," said Iggy, raising his cup.

"So will I!" chorused Arx and Gipsy.

"And I'll drink to *us*," said Teggs, grinning at his fantastic friends. "Here's to the astrosaurs – and to a frantic, fun-filled future for us all!"

INTERVAL

The party went on all night, and Teggs was the last to leave. He stumbled sleepily into his luxury bedroom and flopped onto a huge bed of fresh leaves and straw. He didn't wake up again until late in the afternoon!

"I can't believe I missed breakfast *and* lunch," he murmured, his tum rumbling. "I'd better have three dinners to make up for it!"

He walked to the DSS canteen and saw Gipsy sitting with a cup of fern coffee. "Hello, Captain!" she waved.

"Hi, Gipsy." Teggs helped himself to a steaming pot of stalk stew and sat beside her. "Where are Arx and Iggy?"

"Playing dino-ball with your old
friends from Astrosaurs Academy," Gipsy
informed him. "I said I'd bring you along
when you got up." She smiled. "Blink
and Dutch are great fun, aren't they?"

"They certainly are," Teggs agreed. "So
are Damona and her darlings."

Gipsy frowned. "Her *what*?"

"Netta and Splatt," Teggs explained.
"Their team was Damona's Darlings,

and Dutch, Blink and I were the Daring Dinos."

"You still are, as far as I can see!" said Gipsy. "I bet you had tons of fun together. How did you meet them all?"

"Well . . ." Teggs drained the last of his stew, smacked his lips, and looked into the distance, remembering. "It all started on my very first day at Astrosaurs Academy . . ."

Astrosaurs ACADEMY

STEVE COLE

DESTINATION: DANGER!

Illustrated by Woody Fox

RED FOX

For Tobey and Amy

The cadets

THE DARING DINOS

Teggs   Dutch   Blink

DAMONA'S DARLINGS

Damona   Netta   Splatt

Talking Dinosaur!

How to say the prehistoric names in
DESTINATION: DANGER!

STEGOSAURUS – *STEG-oh-SORE-us*

GRYPOSAURUS – *GRIPE-oh-SORE-us*

DIPLODOCUS – *di-PLOH-de-kus*

IGUANODON – *ig-WA-noh-don*

DICERATOPS – *dye-SERRA-tops*

TRICERATOPS – *try-SERRA-tops*

PTEROSAUR – *teh-roh-SORE*

SEISMOSAURUS – *SIZE-moh-SORE-us*

ANKYLOSAUR – *an-KILE-oh-SORE*

DRYOSAURUS – *DRY-oh-SORE-us*

LAMBEOSAUR – *LAMB-ee-oh-SORE*

SAUROPELTA – *SORE-oh-PEL-ta*

Chapter One

A DINOSAUR'S DREAM

Teggs Stegosaur sat on the back seat of the space-bus, eating his thirty-seventh packed lunch of the day.

And it wasn't even noon yet!

Teggs was a young, orange-brown stegosaurus, who was handsome, bright and very often hungry. He got even hungrier when he was excited . . .

And right now, he was more excited than he had ever been in his life!

"Are we nearly there yet?" Teggs called to the bus driver.

"That's the five hundredth time you've asked," said the bus driver, a grumpy gryposaurus. "And the answer's still no. We only left an hour ago!"

Teggs shrugged and tucked into another sack of apples. As he munched, he stared out of the window at distant stars and comets twinkling in the darkness. He had always dreamed of flying through space, helping other dinosaurs and having adventures. And now, here he was on an empty, rickety old bus hoping to make his dreams come true . . .

It was millions of years since dinosaurs had left behind the planet Earth to start a new life among the stars. Now they lived in a part of space called the Jurassic Quadrant. The plant-eaters lived on one side and the meat-eaters lived on the other.

But sometimes fights broke out, or spooky space monsters attacked, or innocent leaf-munchers needed help. When that happened, special, daring, space-travelling dinosaurs zoomed to the rescue. They belonged to the Dinosaur Space Service and called themselves *astrosaurs*.

More than anything, Teggs wanted to become an astrosaur too. But first I've got to prove I have what it takes, he thought – by training at the Astrosaurs Academy!

"Are we nearly there yet?" Teggs asked yet again.

"*No!*" the driver yelled back, as a large grey planet loomed up in the bus window. "Our next stop is the planet Diplox."

"Diplox," said Teggs, thinking hard. Astrosaurs had to know the names of every planet in the Jurassic Quadrant, as well as the dinosaurs that lived there. "Isn't that where diplodocus come from?"

"Correct," said the driver. He stopped the bus at the orbiting bus stop and opened the doors. "And here comes one now."

A dark green dinosaur wriggled through the bus doors with a huge rucksack on his back. He was short for a diplodocus, but very sturdy. He looked around the bus, his long neck swishing this way and that.

Then he saw Teggs and smiled. "Hey, dude!"

"Hi! I'm Teggs," said Teggs.

"Dutch Delaney," replied the small diplodocus. "Good to meet you, Teggs." He pulled a bat and ball from his rucksack with his mouth. "Do you like sports?"

Teggs grinned. "Let's play!"

Dutch knocked the ball over to Teggs, who whacked it with his spiky tail. But he hit it too hard and it started bouncing all over the bus! "Cool!" cried Dutch, as he dodged the ball with amazing skill.

Finally, the ball hit the driver on the head. "Ow!" he shouted. "No ball games allowed on this bus!"

"Sorry!" Teggs and Dutch called together – but they couldn't help laughing.

"That was a great shot, Teggs," said Dutch admiringly.

Teggs smiled. "That was nice dodging, Dutch!"

"Thanks," said Dutch. "Been on the bus long?"

"Bean? Where's a bean?" Teggs looked

around ravenously, licking his lips.

"No, dude," said Dutch quickly. "I meant, have you been riding this bus a long time?"

"Oh! Only an hour or two," Teggs told him. "I'm on my way to the planet Astro Prime to join—"

"The Astrosaurs Academy!" Dutch beamed. "Me too! Wow, this is awesome." He pulled his 'welcome' letter from his rucksack. "You know, I'm down to share a room with a stegosaurus. I hope he's as cool as you . . ."

"That's funny," said Teggs, looking at his own letter. "I think I'm sharing with a diplodocus . . ."

They both re-read what the letters said — and gasped.

"I'm sharing with *you*!" Teggs cried.

"And me with you!" Dutch happily shook hands with Teggs. "It says we have to share with a flying reptile too."

"Maybe he'll get on at the next stop!" said Teggs, opening up his thirty-eighth packed lunch of apples and ferns. "Would you like something to eat while we're waiting, Dutch?"

"Thanks, dude, but my mum already packed me a snack." Dutch pulled out an enormous, tasty-looking tree from his rucksack. "Want a bite?"

Teggs grinned. "Dutch, I think you might be the perfect roommate. Astrosaurs Academy, here we come!"

Chapter Two

IN TROUBLE ALREADY!

Now Teggs had made friends with
Dutch, the long bus journey seemed to
whizz by. More and more dinosaurs got
on board at every stop, all on their way
to Astrosaurs Academy – but no flying
reptiles were among them. The bus was
bulging with bodies by the time Astro
Prime came in sight!

From a distance, the planet looked
like a red and green
ball floating in
space. But as the
bus zoomed closer
Teggs could see it
was a real patchwork

of places. Huge sweeping deserts mixed with lush jungles. Frozen ice fields gave way to stony sweeps of wilderness. Deep, orange oceans lapped at every different shore.

And on a blue island at the planet's equator stood the Astrosaurs Academy!

 "*Wow*," said Teggs, as he and Dutch peered out of the window. "So this is our new home while we're training!"

The bus soared over the academy, and soon everyone on board was chattering excitedly. It was as if a school had been built in the middle of a massive adventure camp. Teggs's eyes lit up as he saw playing fields, an assault course, a water park and an athletics track, as well as launch pads for spaceships and astro-jets.

Dutch pointed to a huddle of huge wooden huts, hugging the earth like giant woodlice. "What are they?"

Teggs checked his guidebook. "They are the dino-dorms. All the students live there." He pointed to another building. "And there's the best place of all – the canteen!"

The bus landed outside a gleaming metal pyramid. An iguanodon wearing the red uniform of an astrosaur instructor was waiting for them.

"Pay attention, you lot!" the instructor shouted. "Welcome to Astrosaurs Academy. You are just in time – your head teacher, Commander Gruff, is about to speak to all new cadets in the main hall. Grab yourselves a uniform and move out!"

"Let's go!" cried Teggs.

They waved goodbye to the bus driver. Then they ran across the springy blue grass and joined the stream of excited dinosaurs pouring into the pyramid.

The first thing Teggs and Dutch came to was an enormous changing room. Astrosaur cadets wore deep blue tops with 'AA' written on the front and a golden leaf on one sleeve. Clothes flew through the air as every dinosaur tried to find an outfit that fitted.

Proudly
wearing their
new uniforms,
Teggs and
Dutch
followed the
signs to the
main hall.
But when

they got there, they found a crowd
outside listening to a large,
red diceratops. She had two big horns,
three big brown freckles on each cheek
– and one very big mouth!

"Of course, my Uncle
Hiro is a famous
astrosaur
captain," she
said, preening
herself. "He's
taken me to
loads of amazing
planets . . ."

15

"Wow," said a wide-eyed triceratops. "You're so cool, Damona!"

"I was even there when he fought four hundred T. rexes at the Battle of Belliflopp!" Damona went on.

"Really?" A yellow pterosaur with quizzical eyes, glasses and a soft voice hopped up to her. "I read that there were only two hundred T. rexes on Belliflopp."

"Who cares what you read, beak-face?" said Damona hotly. "*I* know because *I* was there. It was definitely four hundred!"

"Then perhaps you can't count!" said Teggs, stepping between them. "I recorded a TV programme about the battle. Your uncle said there was one T. rex hiding on every island in the Belliflopp Sea – making two hundred in total!" He pulled his laptop from his rucksack. "Would you like to watch the show and see?"

Some of the crowd started to snigger. Damona blushed and glared at Teggs. Then she flounced away into the main hall.

"What a silly show-off," said Dutch.

"Maybe it's just her way of making friends," said Teggs, turning to the pterosaur. "I'm Teggs, and this is Dutch. Are you OK?"

"Teggs? Dutch?" The dino-bird, blinked several times, then grinned. "Wow! I think I'm sharing a dino-dorm with you. My name's Blink Fingawing."

"So *you're* our other roommate!" Dutch grinned.

"This is great," said Teggs happily.

Then the ground started to shake under their feet. "Uh-oh. I think Commander Gruff is on his way."

Teggs, Dutch and Blink rushed inside and found some seats in the middle of the hall – just as Commander Gruff

thumped onto
the large stage
at the front. He
was a giant
green
seismosaurus.
Gruff had
fought a
thousand space
battles – and
had the scars to
prove it. But
now he had
retired from the
DSS to teach
young astrosaur
cadets.

"All right, you horrible lot!" he
growled, chewing on an unripe banana
as if it was a cigar. "Right now, you are
simply dinosaurs. But if you train hard,
you might just become *astrosaurs*!"

The cadets clapped loudly.

"You must be brave!" said Commander Gruff. "You must have guts!"

Teggs patted his tummy and smiled at Dutch and Blink. "I've got lots of guts."

"You must be hungry for victory!" Gruff shouted.

Just then, Teggs's tummy gave a huge rumble and the whole hall burst out laughing.

"NO ONE DISTURBS MY SPEECHES!" bellowed Gruff. He stretched his neck all the way to the middle of the hall and glared down at Teggs. "What's your name, cadet?"

"Um . . . Teggs, sir," said Teggs, his heart sinking.

"Get out!" Gruff barked. "I'll see you later."

Teggs felt everyone staring as he got up and plodded from the hall. Damona stuck out her tongue as he passed, and his cheeks blushed bright red. Only here five minutes, he thought, and I'm in trouble already!

But just as he reached the front of the hall, there was an almighty crash above the stage – and part of the ceiling started to fall in!

Commander Gruff jumped away as a giant, struggling monster forced its way through the hole and dropped to the stage below with a *THUMP*. Teggs stared in horror as the monster reared up, roaring with rage and baring its savage teeth . . .

There was a *T. rex* in the heart of the Astrosaurs Academy!

Chapter Three

THE DARING DINOS

Panic broke out in the hall. Dinosaurs jumped up, yelling in alarm as the enormous meat-eater stomped towards them. Commander Gruff reared up to face the T. rex, but it grabbed his neck and threw him to the ground with a *CRASH*.

"Commander!" Teggs yelled. But Gruff didn't move. "Dutch, Blink, look after him. I'll try to hold off the T. rex."

"Everyone out!" shouted Damona, shooing people towards the doors. "Quickly and calmly! No squashing!"

While Damona cleared the hall and Dutch and Blink tried to drag Gruff out of danger, Teggs ran towards the monster. "Take *this*, meathead!" he cried, whacking the T. rex on the knee with his spiky tail.

The T. rex growled and tried to bite Teggs – but then a speeding baseball bounced off its nose and stopped it in its tracks.

"Got you!" Dutch whooped. He pulled more baseballs from his rucksack and started lobbing them at the monster's head.

Meanwhile, Blink flew up into the air. He flapped around like a mad moth with wind, pecking the T. rex in the ear. At the same time, Teggs stamped on its foot. The T. rex didn't know who to squish first!

"Hey! I've found a wire in its ear!"
yelled Blink, tugging out a bright red
lead. Sparks began to fly from the
monster's eyeballs.

"It must be a robot!" Teggs realized.
"But where did it come from?"

"Out of my way, you lot," said Damona. She had finished getting everyone outside. Now she lowered her horns and charged at the sparking T. rex. *WHAM!* She hit it so hard that both its legs fell off! With a clanking, clanging *KER-KROOM!* the robot broke down.

"Well done, Damona!" said Teggs.

"That was some charge!"

"It was, wasn't it?" she agreed. "I suppose you were quite brave too."

"You all were," said Commander Gruff, getting up again. "Well done, cadets.

You handled that exercise very well."

"Exercise?" Teggs echoed.

"I *love* exercise!" said Dutch.

"The commander means it was just a test, silly!" said Damona.

"Exactly," Gruff agreed. "The first thing I do with any new group of cadets is test how they respond to deadly danger."

Blink polished his glasses on his wing. "I suppose that if you want to be an astrosaur, you must expect the unexpected!"

"Too right." Gruff turned to Damona. "You got everyone out double-quick, cadet. Now let's see you get them back in again!"

"Yes, sir!" Damona saluted, then ran out to round up the other students.

"And as for you, Teggs . . ." Gruff pulled a clump of ferns from the wall and gave them to him.

"Keep your tummy rumbles under control and sit back down."

Teggs scoffed the ferns, saluted and went back to his seat with Blink and Dutch. "Phew!" he said.

Soon all the cadets were back inside, staring at the wreck of the robot T. rex.

"That was just a little test of your bravery," Gruff growled. "And let me tell you – if you ever meet a *real* T. rex, screaming and shouting will *not* help you!" He chomped some more on his unripe banana. "Now it's time to talk about your first mission."

Blink blinked excitedly. "Wow! A mission already!"

"As you know, astrosaurs are excellent explorers – and so must you be," Gruff bellowed. "SO! You will get into teams of three. First thing tomorrow morning you will be taken to the land of Quarrik. It is a deserted wilderness. Each team must build a camp and then go off to explore. To win your Planet Explorer medals, you must find something extraordinary and rare and bring it back to the academy for a show-and-tell. The best one will win a special award."

"How long do we have, sir?" called Damona.

"Twenty-four hours," said Gruff. "You will camp out overnight and an astro-jet will pick you up the next morning. But until then you will be completely on your own."

"Awesome!" whispered Dutch, and

Teggs and Blink both nodded.

"Class dismissed," said Gruff. "But before you go, you horrible lot . . . you can clean up the mess this robot made and fix that hole in the roof!"

Later, tired and covered in dust and dirt, Teggs, Blink and Dutch staggered back to the dino-dorms. Their room was large but quite bare. The only furniture was two beds and a large nest, three desks, three wardrobes, a couch and a fridge.

"The fridge could be larger," said Teggs.

"Eh?" Blink blinked. "It's the size of a shuttle!"

"Exactly!" said Dutch. "But we've got *starship*-sized appetites!"

"Well, we had better get unpacking." Teggs struggled to pull a large bush out of his bag. "I've got so much food in here I should call it a ruck*snack*!"

"I'll give you a hand," said Dutch. He took an enormous leafy bite. "Or do I mean a mouth!"

"Hey!" Teggs grinned. "Save me a bit. Go and eat Blink's grub."

"Yes, I've got a nice crunchy bug salad here," said Blink. He stuck his beak in a lunchbox and sucked up a big pile of speckled leaves and deep-fried insects.

"Mmm! Care for a pickled earwig?"

Dutch pulled a face. "Maybe I'll pass."

The three new friends explored the rest of the room. Blink flapped into his nest and neatly arranged each stray stick.

Teggs bounced on his bed, testing the springs.

Meanwhile, Dutch opened his bag and started chucking his clothes carelessly over his shoulder.

A huge pair of pants landed on Blink's head. "Oof!" he twittered. "What are you doing?"

"Unpacking, dude," said Dutch.

"But you're making such a mess!" Blink grinned. "Brilliant! I love sorting out messes!" And as Dutch went on emptying his bag, Blink swooped about the room, catching things and folding them neatly. "I think I'm definitely going to like it here," he cried, blinking busily away. "New uniforms, new friends . . . and we've had our first battle already!"

"Speaking of the battle," said Teggs. "I thought we made a pretty good team against that robot. So I was wondering . . ."

"Would we like to be on your team for the mission tomorrow?" Blink looked at Dutch and they both nodded. "Yes, please!"

"That would be way cool!" Dutch added.

"Excellent!" said Teggs, jumping off the bed. "I bet we will find something amazing in the wilderness."

Dutch nodded. "And build a brilliant camp too!"

"But what shall we call ourselves?" Blink wondered.

"I know," Teggs declared. "The Daring Dinos!"

"*Awwwwwwesome!*" roared Dutch. "Now let's celebrate by eating ten dinners in the canteen!" He held out his hand. "Do we dare?"

Teggs and Blink put their hands on top of his and they all shouted together: "WE DARE!"

Whooping, the Daring Dinos raced outside. As they ran over the blue grass, Teggs saw a shooting star fall from the sky. His mum had always said you were supposed to wish on a falling star, so Teggs did.

"I wish that the Planet Explorer mission tomorrow is the wildest mission ever!" he said.

The shooting star lingered in the sky for a few moments, almost as if it was listening. Then it dropped out of sight behind the distant mountains.

Little did Teggs know that his wish was going to come true – but not in a way that anyone could expect . . .

Chapter Four

JOURNEY TO PERIL

At sunrise the next day, all the astrosaur cadets trooped down to the launch pads to collect their camping kits and get on the astro-jets.

Blink was super-excited. He was zipping about like a budgie with a firework up its bottom. "A mission!" he cried. "Our very first astro-tastic mission!"

Teggs grinned through a yawn. He had spent most of the night checking his alarm clock to see if it was time to get up yet. He couldn't wait to get started.

Dutch had barely slept either. Now he was actually sleepwalking to the astro-jets, snoring like an elephant!

Suddenly, a pink ankylosaur with a blue bow tied around her big, club-like tail sneaked up behind him and shouted, "BOO!"

Dutch jumped in the air in surprise, and his rucksack fell off his back. It landed on Teggs's toe. "*Ow!*"

Teggs and Dutch both glared at the ankylosaur, whose bumpy body quivered as she giggled away. Damona walked up to her with a big smile. "Good trick, Netta. You really made the diplodocus jump!"

"I'll make you jump in a minute!" Dutch retorted.

But suddenly, a small, nimble boy dinosaur with the head of a turtle and the tail of a snake went zooming over Dutch's back and made him jump again! Damona and Netta laughed even louder. "Nice one, Splatt!"

"So this is *your* team, is it, Damona?" asked Teggs.

"Meet Damona's Darlings," she replied. "Netta is super-strong and Splatt is a super-speedy dryosaurus. We are going to be the best team at Astrosaurs Academy."

"No contest!" said Splatt, whizzing around Dutch in a circle.

Dutch tried to sit on him, but missed and sat on a big thistle. "*Ouch!*"

Blink came flapping down beside Damona. "I think you'll find that we are the best team, actually," he said proudly. "The Daring Dinos!"

"The Dino Dimwits, more like!" Damona laughed. She walked off with Netta and Splatt. "See you in the wilderness, boys!"

Dutch scowled. "Dudes, I think those three could be trouble."

"Good." Teggs grinned. "I *like* trouble." He put an arm round Blink and his tail round Dutch. "Now, let's get on board and get ready to win that special prize. Do we dare?"

"WE DARE!" they yelled together.

The astro-jets took off and soared away through the bright blue sky. In minutes, the academy was just a speck in the distance.

The dinosaurs were all squashed in together with their camping kits, ready to parachute down to the surface once they reached the drop zone. They flew over an orange sea and a range of purple mountains. Then Teggs saw the land beneath them grow grey and grotty. Soon there was nothing to see but bare hillsides and stony plains and the occasional twisted tree.

"We have now reached the land of
Quarrik," Blink announced like a tour
guide. "I read about it in a book. It's five
hundred miles north of the academy,
west of the Backplate Sea. There are
loads of really interesting caves—"

"Put a sock in your beak!" called
Netta, and some of the cadets laughed.

Blink looked sad.

"Don't worry about them, Blink," said Teggs. "If they don't want to know that's their problem. What else is in Quarrik?"

"There are some very steep cliffs and very deep valleys," Blink went on, perking up a bit. "I hope we get to explore some of those!"

The astro-jet started to slow down and a red light flashed above their heads. "I think we've reached the drop zone," Teggs realized.

"And I want to jump first!" Dutch declared, as a hatch opened up in the side of the jet. He lumbered over and jumped out without a second thought. "*Awwwwwwwwve-soooooome!*" he yelled.

"Me next!" cried Damona and Teggs together. They squeezed out through the hatch and dived into empty space.

"*Whoaaaa!*" yelled Teggs in delight.

Here he was – a
six-ton stegosaurus
– flying like
a dino-bird!
Soon, the sky
was full of
dinosaurs plunging
downwards.
They opened their
parachutes and
floated to earth
as gently as leaves
in the autumn.

"*Wow!*" Teggs shouted, as he hit the ground beside Dutch. The parachute fell over him like a stripy cloak. "Let's do it again!"

"No time for that," squawked Blink, landing beside them. He hadn't needed a parachute, of course. "We must find a cool place to camp."

Already, the other cadets were zooming over the wasteland, as busy as ants, hunting about for the best places. Blink led the way up a hill, poking his beak here and there. "I'm glad I read that guidebook now. Somewhere around here there's a really good cave . . ."

Teggs bounded to the top of the hill. "How about this one?" he said.

Blink flapped over to see. "That's it! This will give us extra shelter."

Dutch beamed. "And it's close to that little stream for drinking water and washing too! Top work, Blink!"

But suddenly, they heard a cry for help from further down the hill. "Somebody . . . come quick!"

Dutch frowned. "That sounds like Damona!"

Teggs pointed. "There!"

Damona was lying under a fallen tree. Netta was struggling to lift it so her friend could get free.

"Looks like she's in trouble," yelled Teggs. "Come on!"

Chapter Five

A DEADLY DISCOVERY

Teggs ran down the hill to help, with Blink and Dutch close behind. "Damona, are you all right?"

"Yes, thanks!" She sucked in her tummy and wriggled out from under the tree. "Fancy that! I seem to have got out all by myself . . ."

"And *I've* found a *brilliant* place to camp!" called Splatt from the top of the hill. He put down his self-inflating tent right outside the cave Teggs had just spotted!

"Unfair, dude," said Dutch crossly. "We were there first!"

"You should have stayed there then, shouldn't you?" Damona and Netta waved and laughed. "So long, see you, wouldn't want to be you!"

Blink blinked furiously. "The cheats!"

Dutch scowled. "That was *our* camp."

"Oh, let them have it," said Teggs. He turned and walked off in the opposite direction. "I bet we'll find a much better place to camp over here."

50

"Maybe." Blink didn't seem sure. "The guidebook says there are lots of steep cliffs and deep valleys this way."

"Well, we're bound to find some brilliant things for show-and-tell as we go," said Dutch. "Keep your eyes peeled, Blink!"

Blink flew on ahead, circling above the trees and peeping behind big rocks. But it seemed all the best places had been taken.

"Look! There's a giant pine cone!" Dutch picked it up. "Pretty unusual, huh?"

"I've seen two teams with giant pine cones already," said Blink.

Dutch tried again. "What about this funny-shaped twig?"

"I've seen *three* teams with funny-shaped twigs."

They rambled onwards, for hours and hours, until they were far away from everyone else. They scrambled up steep slopes and splashed through muddy mountain streams.

Teggs paused by a tree full of hazelnuts. "What about these?"

Blink frowned. "Nuts? For show-and-tell?"

"No, for a snack!" said Teggs, shaking

the tree and catching the nuts in his mouth. "I'm starving!"

They plodded along beside a cliff edge then took a winding woodland path. A cold wind started to blow up. It whistled eerily through the branches of the twisted trees. The howls of strange creatures echoed in the distance.

Dutch gulped, a little bit spooked. "I don't like this."

"Maybe we should make a camp right here," Teggs suggested.

Blink quickly agreed. "I have a feeling there's something really unusual around here just waiting to be discovered."

"Yeah!" said Dutch. He pulled an orange inflatable bundle from his rucksack and laid it on the ground.

"Luckily it won't take long to set up camp. These tents are self-inflating – all you do is pull the string and up they go!"

He bent over
the bundle and
yanked on a long
black cord. The
tent puffed up
in moments to
the size of a
garage. But
then a strong
gust of wind caught it and the tent blew
away!

"Oh, no!" yelled Dutch. "My tent! I
can't sleep without it, my
toes will freeze off!"

"Come on,
Dutch," said
Blink,
flapping
his
leathery
wings. "I'll
help you
catch it!"

"I'll stay here and get the campfire going," Teggs told them. "Good luck!"

The squashy orange tent was blown tumbling through the sky like an oversized kite. Dutch charged after it, crashing through bracken and leaping over rocks. Blink flapped his wings and tried to overtake it.

"Quickly!" the pterosaur cried. "It looks like the edge of the cliff up ahead. If the tent blows over there we'll never get it back!"

Dutch broke into a gallop. Stretching his neck as far as it would go, he grabbed hold of the runaway tent with his teeth. At the same time, Blink dive-bombed it, pinning it to the ground with his claws – just before it reached the cliff edge.

"Thanks, dude!" said Dutch, spitting out his rubbery mouthful. "That was close!"

"Shh!" said Blink, sniffing the air. "What's that horrible smell?"

"It's not me!" Dutch grinned. "Whoever smelt it, dealt it!"

"I'm serious." Blink's beak was twitching. "Yuck! It smells like maggots and muck and mouldy barbecues . . ."

"And it's coming from over the cliff edge," Dutch realized.

Cautiously, the two friends crept over to the ledge to see. And what they saw chilled their blood.

A small crimson spaceship had crashed in the valley below. Six huge, evil-looking monsters in dark tatty clothes were stamping through the wreckage. Their legs were huge but their arms were tiny. The cold sunlight caught on their claws and their rows of knife-sharp teeth.

Both Dutch and Blink recognized the monsters at once.

T. rexes!

Chapter Six

THE TRICK AND THE T. REX

"This can't be happening!" Dutch stared at Blink. "What are T. rexes doing on Astro Prime?"

"Maybe Commander Gruff is testing us again," Blink whispered hopefully. "Maybe they're robots like before!"

But suddenly, they heard the tallest T. rex speak in an angry roar. "Will ship fly again, pilot?"

"No, Lord Slyme," growled a T. rex in flying goggles. "Ship completely stuffed."

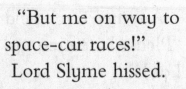

"But me on way to space-car races!" Lord Slyme hissed. "Now me have to miss them. Me go back to spaceship shop and EAT owner for selling me pile of scrap!"

"First us must call rescue ship from Teerex Major," said another T. rex.

Dutch gulped. "Dude, I don't think those things are Gruff's robots. They're meat, not metal."

Blink nodded nervously. "I read that a T. rex noble-saur always travels with five servants. Their spaceship must have gone off course and crashed here!"

"Me STARVING," roared Slyme suddenly.

Another T. rex held up an arm. "Please be eating my unworthy elbow, Lord."

But Slyme swatted his servant's arm away. "No!" He sniffed the air, looking

 up towards where Blink and Dutch were hiding. "Me smell fresh, soft meat . . . Nice smell, coming from south . . . Us find."

Shaking with fear, Blink and Dutch slithered away out of sight.

"What can we do?" hissed Dutch. "If those things go south, they will sniff out the cadets' campsites for sure."

"We must tell Teggs," said Blink, blinking so fast his eyelids were a blur through his glasses. "Together we can work out a plan . . . I hope!"

Teggs was just collecting firewood when
Dutch and Blink came hurtling towards
him, dragging the torn tent between
them. They were red-faced, wild-eyed
and gasping for breath. Dutch panted so
hard he blew away Teggs's pile of sticks!

"What's up?" Teggs asked.

"What's *down*, you mean," puffed
Blink, fanning his hot face with his
wing. "A T. rex ship, to be precise!"

Dutch nodded. "There are six real live
T. rexes on our doorstep!"

"*What . . . ?*" Struck dumb with amazement, Teggs listened as his friends revealed all they had seen and heard.

"That shooting star I saw last night," he remembered. "It must have been the T. rex ship crash-landing here." Teggs jumped to his feet. "Everyone in Quarrik is in terrible danger!"

"We can't even get help," Blink twittered. "The astro-jet isn't picking us up until tomorrow morning."

"Then we will just have to help ourselves," Teggs declared. He thought hard. "We must try to scare those monsters away – or at least slow them down."

Dutch gulped. "I guess all we can do is try, right?"

"Right." Teggs looked at the ripped, rubbery orange tent and began to smile. "Tell me, guys, have you ever met the Dreaded Eight-Legged Rock-Spitting Blob Monster?"

"Er, no," Blink admitted, and Dutch shook his head.

"Neither have I," said Teggs. "But I think it's time those T. rexes did!" Teggs grinned at his puzzled friends. "Blink, you're the fastest. Fly back to the camp and warn everyone. They must clear out double-quick."

"OK, Teggs," said Blink, blinking like crazy.

"While you're gone, Dutch and I will turn this tent into a creepy costume," Teggs explained. "We will dress up as a Rock-Spitting Blob Monster!"

"Wow," Dutch gasped. "That plan rocks!"

Blink shook his head. "You mean, that plan *spits* rocks – at the T. rexes!"

"Right!" Teggs looked at his two friends. "We've got a deadly dangerous job to do, dinos . . . Do we dare?"

Blink and Dutch put their own hands on top of Teggs's. "WE DARE!" they all cried.

As Blink flapped away at top speed, Teggs picked up the orange tent. "I'll get to work on this," he said. "Dutch, go and collect some rocks, as big as you can carry."

"Will do," said Dutch. "Let's hope those scaly suckers get such a fright, they run far away from the camp and never come back!"

Soon, Dutch and Teggs were struggling into the home-made monster suit. Teggs had dug up some chalk and mud and used it to draw a frightening face on one end of the deflated rubber. Then he had cut out some eyeholes to see through and also a flap so they could throw rocks at their unwelcome visitors. The rocks were balanced between the spikes on Teggs's back so Dutch could reach them easily.

"Do you think we look scary enough?" said Dutch.

"Don't forget, we will also be roaring, spitting rocks and running about on eight legs," said Teggs. "What could be scarier? Let's get going!"

Reaching the right place wasn't easy. It was hot and squashed inside the costume. Teggs and Dutch couldn't see very well, so they kept tripping up and walking into trees. The wind almost knocked them over several times. The rocks on Teggs's back made his spikes ache.

"T. rex valley coming up," Dutch whispered at last. "They were right at the bottom when we left them . . ."

But suddenly, Teggs saw movement in the undergrowth ahead. The butterflies in his tummy turned into bats as six savage T. rexes burst from the bushes! They stared in surprise at the orange blobby monster in front of them.

"They must have climbed out!" Dutch whispered.

"Quick, make like a monster," said Teggs. "ROOAAAAAAR!" he bellowed. Dutch snatched some rocks from Teggs's back and threw them out of the mouth-flap. "GRROO AAARRR!" The two of them stamped about in their costume, growling till their throats hurt.

The T. rexes just stood there.

"Lord Slyme!" growled the T. rex in flying goggles. "Me thinks us find eight-legged rock-spitting blob monster!"

Lord Slyme snapped his jaws. "Good. Now us *eat* it!"

With a hungry hiss, the terrifying giants stomped towards Teggs and Dutch . . .

Chapter Seven

RACE AGAINST TIME

Terribly tired and scared out of his scales, Blink flew on towards the main camp through the driving wind. "Can't give up," he told himself. "Mustn't give up . . ."

Finally, he flapped out of the sky and flopped down in front of Damona's cave, gasping for breath.

"Clear out!" he squawked.

"Beak-face?" Damona poked her two-horned head out of the cave and frowned. "What are you doing back? Did you get lost?"

"Get everyone out of the camp," the dino-bird panted. "T. rexes close by!"

"T. rexes?" Damona looked shocked. Netta and Splatt peeped out from behind her.

"Teggs and Dutch are risking their lives right now, trying to scare them away," Blink explained. "But that might not work. Everyone must pack up and head north, quickly!"

"Oh, *I* get it . . ." Damona started to smirk. "Nice try, Blink."

Netta nodded. "You can stop pretending now."

"Pretending?" Blink blinked at her furiously. "I'm telling the truth! There *are* T. rexes here!"

"As if," said Splatt. "You're just trying to scare us out so you can get this cool cave back."

"Who cares about a dumb cave?" Blink squawked.

"You do," said Damona. "Now push off!"

"You have to believe me, you two-horned twit!" Blink shouted. Then he flapped down the hillside to where a trio of triceratops sat beneath a tree.

"Please, guys, listen. We have to clear the camp, quickly. There are T. rexes—"

"Don't listen to him!" Netta yelled. "He's trying to pinch your camp for himself."

"I'm not!" Blink protested.

But the three triceratops gave him a dirty look and stalked away.

Desperately, Blink hopped over to a lime-coloured lambeosaur. "Will you help me clear the camp before the T. rexes sniff it out?"

"T. rexes indeed," the lambeosaur said stuffily.

Blink flapped up and down helplessly. "No one will believe me!" he cried. "Oh, help. What am I going to do?"

"CATCH ORANGE MONSTER THING! *EAT IT!*"

Lord Slyme's screech echoed through the air as Teggs and Dutch hurtled through the wilderness in their tattered tent costume. Teggs's heart was pounding. His mouth was dry. A stitch burned in his side. But he wouldn't stop running, and neither would Dutch.

Trouble was, the drooling T. rexes wouldn't stop either. Which meant that Teggs and Dutch would end up leading them straight to the cadet camp! Every time they tried to change direction, another of the ravenous 'rexes mashed through the spindly undergrowth and blocked their way, forcing them back onto the main path.

"What do we do?" Dutch panted, as they ran along the edge of a cliff. "If we get too tired, we get eaten!"

Teggs grinned weakly. "Let's not get too tired!"

Ahead of them, the cliff path curved sharply past a huge boulder. But as they took the turn, Dutch stumbled and slipped out of the costume – and over the cliff edge!

"Dutch!" Teggs yelled, skidding to a stop.

"It's OK!" Dutch's head popped back into view. "There's a ledge down here. We can hide till they go past!"

Teggs jumped down to join Dutch, who hid inside the costume again – just as the hunting T. rexes raced round the corner and pounded past. They did not realize their prey had given them the slip.

"Phew!" said Dutch.

"But those meatheads are still heading for the camp," Teggs reminded him. "I only hope Blink has got the cadets clear by now—Whoops!"

Suddenly, a big gust of wind blew under the tent and knocked them both off the ledge!

"Looks like we're going for an unexpected trip," cried Dutch. "*Whoooaaaa!*"

Helpless, the two friends tumbled down the steep slope of the cliff. Luckily, the tent-costume's rubbery material protected them from the worst bumps. With a roll, a bump, two triple somersaults and a thump, they finally reached the bottom.

"What a ride," groaned Dutch, shaking off bits of tent. "Even my bruises have bruises."

"But look," said Teggs shakily, pointing past a clump of trees. "I think we found a shortcut . . ."

On the other side of the trees were a dozen more bright orange tents. It was the cadet camp!

"Come on!" Dutch pulled Teggs back to his feet and they limped towards it. But when they arrived, they couldn't believe their eyes. Everyone was still here! Some dinosaurs were exploring, some were reading, some were toasting marshmallows without a care in the world.

And there was Blink, flapping about like crazy. "The T. rexes *are* coming!" he kept squawking. "It's true!"

"Yes, it is!" Teggs yelled.

Suddenly, everyone stopped what they were doing and stared.

"Teggs, I'm so sorry!" said Blink,
flapping over to his side. "No one will
listen. Damona told everyone I was
playing a trick to get our cave back!"

Even as he spoke, Damona strolled
out of the cave and noticed Teggs and
Dutch. "Hey, what happened to you

two?" she called. "You look awful! You look like you went ten rounds with a . . ." Her face went pale. "With a *T. rex*?"

"Six of them, to be precise," said Teggs gravely. "They are very big and very fast – and they will be here any minute!"

Chapter Eight

THE BIG, FAT BATTLE

"You heard Teggs," Dutch shouted at the astrosaur cadets. "We need to get out of here, dudes. *Scram!*"

The cadets stared at Teggs and Dutch in alarm and amazement. Then they burst into action, deflating their tents and packing up their camps.

Damona came running up to Teggs with Netta and Splatt. "I'm sorry," she said. "I thought you were playing a joke on us. Blink would have got everyone safely away long ago if it wasn't for me."

"Never mind that now," said Teggs. "You were super-fast at clearing everyone out of the hall yesterday. Do you think you can do the same here?"

"I'll do it even *faster* with my team to help me," Damona promised.

Netta and
Splatt were
already on the
case. "Come on,
you lot!" boomed
Netta, while
Splatt whizzed
about like a
sheepdog herding
sheep. "You can

all hide in our cave. It's very deep."

"I'm not sure that will work!" said
Blink, blinking. "I've read all about T.
rexes. Once those meat-scoffing
monsters smell a meal, they won't rest
till they've eaten it. Our only chance is
to run away and stay far enough ahead
of them!"

"Maybe not our *only* chance,"
breathed Teggs. He was watching
one of the plump orange tents deflate.
It went from a bungalow-sized balloon
to a fat lump of rubber in seconds.

"I've got an idea — but it's very, very dangerous. Who will help me stand up to those monsters?"

"I will," said Dutch.

"And me!" trilled Blink.

Damona stepped forward. "My uncle sorted out the T. rexes, and so will I!"

Teggs called out to the camp. "OK, I need two more volunteers."

A large, grey triceratops called Trebor and a gum-chewing girl sauropelta called Akk broke away from the line of dinosaurs queuing at the cave. "We will help too," Trebor said.

"I'll organize everyone in the cave," Splatt offered.

86

"And we will be standing by to help you if things go wrong," Netta promised.

"OK, guys," said Teggs. "Here's what we do . . ."

Five minutes later, Teggs and his helpers were waiting nervously for their face-off with the ravenous 'rexes. Teggs wasn't sure he would hear them coming over the pounding of his heart.

"My uncle fought T. rexes with dung-torpedoes and laser-blasters at the Battle of Belliflop." Damona sighed and looked down at the bright, rubbery bundles in her arms. "What have we got? Tents!"

"You know what to do," Teggs murmured.

"Yes." Blink clutched a small pile of deflated tents to his chest. "And our timing must be perfect."

Dutch nodded. "A second too late and it's, 'Hello, T. rex tum' time!"

Suddenly, they felt the ground tremble under their feet, and heard heavy footsteps crashing towards them.

"Good luck, everyone," Teggs whispered.

The next moment, with an ear-splitting roar, all six T. rexes smashed through the nearby bushes. At the sight of the plant-eaters their piggy eyes grew wide as saucers. Their little arms twitched. Their big jaws dribbled.

Lord Slyme pushed to the front of the scaly scrum. "What have us here?" he hissed. "A juicy jumble of jelly-soft dino-dinners! Me a *brilliant* hunter!"

"Brilliant?" Teggs scoffed, as Slyme stamped towards him. "I think you've got an *inflated* opinion of yourself!"

The horrible hunter opened his jaws to bite him in half. But Teggs hurled the tent into Slyme's mouth and yanked on the black cord. The tent puffed up in a moment – and so did Slyme's throat!

"*MRRRRPH!*" he spluttered, his little arms waving in the air. It looked as if he had swallowed a space-hopper!

Angrily – but also stupidly – the other T. rexes attacked in the same way. Dutch dumped his tent in the mouth of one of them and yanked on the cord. Its head inflated like a big balloon!

Another tried to catch Blink. But Blink flapped into the air. As the T. rex looked up, Blink dropped three tents down its neck and pulled the strings. The monster's stomach swelled up and it bounced about helplessly.

Trebor dealt with another T. rex just as Dutch had. But Akk was not so lucky. Her tent inflated by accident before she could get it into anyone's mouth. Two 'rexes charged towards her . . .

"Teggs!" shouted Damona. "Let's play skittles!"

Teggs took one look at the T. rex with the round, inflated tummy and understood what she meant. Together, the two cadets whacked the evil hunter with their tails. They sent it rolling like a giant, scaly bowling ball! It knocked over the two T. rexes before they could grab Akk. Akk quickly jumped on their heads and knocked them senseless.

That left just one T. rex standing. But it was the fastest of all. It darted forward and sank its teeth into Teggs's tail!

"*Yeeeowwww!*" Teggs yelled, as powerful jaws lifted him into the air . . .

"All charge!" yelled Dutch.

He, Damona, Trebor and Akk ran at the T. rex at the same time. They smashed into its scaly stomach and sides. The T. rex gasped. Teggs slipped from its jaws and tumbled to the ground. At the same moment, Blink swooped down and chucked another two saggy tents into the monster's mouth.

"*URRPH!*" spluttered the T. rex. Its
jaws were yanked open as the tents
inflated, and its eyes nearly popped from
its head! It staggered back, tripped over
Lord Slyme's oversized neck and crashed
to the floor.

"We beat them!" cried Trebor,
grabbing Akk in a hug.

"But what about Teggs?" cried Blink. "He's not moving!"

Blink, Dutch and Damona raced to the stegosaur's side. But was it too late . . . ?

Chapter Nine

A SNAPPY SOUVENIR

"Dude!" Dutch crouched over Teggs.
"Wake up. Your plan totally worked!"
  "Please wake up," Blink added.
"You're the most daring dino of all. You
can't leave us!"

"Yeah, come on, you dumb, brave stegosaur," said Damona, nudging his cheek with her horns. "You *must* be all right. If you're not, I will never forgive you!"

Teggs's eyes flickered open. "I . . . I . . ."

"He's alive!" Blink turned a somersault. "Yay!"

"Shh," said Damona, straining to hear. "He's trying to say something."

"I . . . think . . ." Teggs raised his head weakly to look at her – then grinned. "I think you're standing on my foot!"

"Teggs!" She scowled, backing away. "I thought you were hurt."

"I'm fine now!" Teggs cried, bouncing up and hugging his friends. "Apart from some tooth-marks in my tail. Well done, all of you."

"Hooray!" yelled Netta, leading the other cadets from the cave. They all burst into applause.

"You've turned T. rex into T. *wrecks*!" Splatt cried, dancing round the scaly monsters as they lay groaning on the ground. "Let's tie them up, quickly."

Damona frowned. "But we don't have any ropes."

"Then we must find some," said Teggs. "All of us!"

The cadets worked
as a team. Some dug
up tough tree roots.
Some went to their
first-aid kits and
knotted bandages
together. The T. rexes
only had small arms
so they were quite easy to tie up. One
lambeosaur even found a giant snake! It
coiled itself around Lord
Slyme's legs and arms
very happily, gripping
them tight. The
T. rex wriggled
helplessly in the
serpent's grip.

"No one treats
me like this,"
snarled Lord
Slyme with some
difficulty. "No
one!"

"*We* do," said Teggs. "The cadets of Astrosaurs Academy!"

Suddenly, the sound of huge engines filled the air. Everyone stared in astonishment as a giant craft swished down from the sky.

"It's the astro-jet!" Teggs yelled, as the mighty space-plane landed close by.

A moment later, Commander Gruff stuck his head out through the doors, an unripe banana clamped in his mouth as always. "Looks like you new recruits had a little trouble here."

"Nothing we couldn't handle, sir," said Teggs, smiling at Damona.

"We worked together and got the job done," Damona agreed. "Although obviously *I* was best—" Dutch nudged her in the ribs. "Ow!"

"How come you came back for us early, sir?" asked Blink.

"When those T. rexes crashed they sent a call for help to their home planet," Gruff revealed.

"Right!' Dutch turned to Blink. "We heard them say they would, remember?"

"Well, we picked up their signal and came flying to get them," said Gruff. "But it seems we wasted our time!"

"I don't think so, sir," said Teggs, smiling at his friends. "The sooner this lot get off Astro Prime, the better!"

"Us agree," moaned the T. rex with the inflated stomach. "Us *definitely* agree!"

Commander Gruff took charge and things were soon sorted out. Lord Slyme and his slaves were sent back to Teerex Major with a warning never to return to plant-eater space. And more astro-jets arrived to take Teggs and all his fellow cadets back to Astrosaurs Academy.

Teggs was exhausted. He slept for twenty-four hours. When he woke up his tail was throbbing – but otherwise he felt fine. In fact he was so hungry he ate his mattress! Then he, Blink and Dutch went to the Learning Zone for their afternoon class.

"Oh, no!" Blink squawked.

"What's up, dude?" Dutch wondered.

He shook his beak. "In all the excitement, we never got anything for show-and-tell!"

"Bad luck, Teggs!" Damona smirked. "Looks like you might not be getting your Planet Explorer's medal after all!"

Teggs's heart sank. "Damona's right. We haven't completed our mission!"

Netta giggled, and Splatt pulled out a giant pine cone from under his desk. "We brought back this. It's bound to win the special prize!"

Just then, Commander Gruff stomped into the classroom. Everyone saluted.

"OK," Gruff said impatiently. "You had some unexpected action in your camp yesterday, but it's time to get back to business. We will start with show-and-tell."

"Oh, no!" groaned Dutch.

Every team had something to show. Damona's Darlings had their giant pine cone. The Triceratops Troop produced a perfect pink eggshell. The Leaf-Loving Squad pulled out a funny-shaped stick . . . and so it went on.

"Hmm, not bad," said Gruff, as Trebor showed off a fossil spider. "And what about the Daring Dinos? What have *you* got?"

"Um . . ." Blink blinked so hard he blew some paper off his desk. "We seem to have . . . accidentally . . . er . . ."

"Forgotten to get anything," Dutch concluded.

You could have heard a pin drop in the quiet classroom. Teggs felt dreadful.

Gruff cleared his throat. "You were very brave in the wilderness, boys, and I am proud of you all." He sighed. "But I cannot break the rules. If you did not bring back anything to show and tell, you have failed the mission – and I cannot give you your Planet Explorer medals."

"Wait!" squawked Blink. And he pecked at the bony barbs at the end of Teggs's tail.

"Ow!" Teggs yelped. "What was that for?"

Dutch grinned. "Looks like you *did* bring something back after all, dude!"

Blink opened his beak – and Teggs saw a large, ivory spike lying there. He grinned. "A T. rex tooth! It must have got stuck in my tail when that monster bit me."

"Cool!" cried Trebor, and the rest of the class joined in with *oohs* and *ahhs*.

"I suppose it's *quite* a good show-and-tell," said Damona huffily. But then she managed a smile. "OK. It's brilliant."

"Indeed it is!" Commander Gruff grinned. "In fact – it's going to win the special prize – a whole starship full of fresh food to chomp on."

"*Wheeeee!*" cried Blink, as Dutch gave him and Teggs a high-five.

"And everyone can join in the feast," Teggs declared. "We will have a party in the dino-dorms tonight!" Damona, Netta and Splatt led the cheering that followed, and Teggs beamed round at his fellow cadets. "We've made it through our first mission at Astrosaurs Academy . . . and I can't wait to find out what we'll be getting up to next!"

THE END

ASTRO PUZZLE TIME

EARTH ATTACK!
QUIZ Questions

1. What does DSS stand for?

2. What did Zindi Bent invent?

3. What is an exo-suit and what does it do?

4. How did Loki and the Astrosaurs reach Earth so quickly?

5. What did Gipsy and Teggs do to disguise themselves when they reached carnivore camp?

6. What flavour coffee did Gipsy drink in the DSS canteen?

Answers:

1. Dinosaur Space Service

2. She invented a time machine

3. Part-costume, part-machine, it allows the wearer to travel through time safely

4. They went through a space tunnel

5. They used sharp stones for fangs and Teggs disguised his backplates with mud

6. Fern Coffee

ASTRO PUZZLE TIME

All this time travel has made things change a little. Can you spot the five differences between these images?

ABOUT THE AUTHOR

Photo: Rebecca Judge.com

Steve Cole has now written fifty books published by Random House Children's Books. As well as the hugely popular *Astrosaurs* and *Astrosaurs Academy* series, he is also the author of *Cows in Action* and *Slime Squad*, and the *Z. Rex* and *Tripwire* sequences for older readers.

Steve has also written lots of other books for different publishers, including several *Doctor Who* novels which have become UK bestsellers. He has also been the editor of fiction and non-fiction titles.

Steve lives in Buckinghamshire with his wife and two children. You can find out more about him at

www·stevecolebooks·co·uk

Visit www.**stevecolebooks**.co.uk for fun, games, jokes, to meet the characters and much, much more!

Welcome to a world where dinosaurs fly spaceships and cows use a time-machine . . .

Sign up for the free Steve Cole monthly newsletter to find out what your favourite author is up to!

There are lots more Steve Cole books for you to try. Take a peek at some of these . . .

Meet the time-travelling cows!

THE TER-MOO-NATORS

BY STEVE COLE

IT'S 'UDDER' MADNESS!

Genius cow Professor McMoo and his trusty sidekicks, Pat and Bo, are the star agents of the C.I.A. –short for COWS IN ACTION! They travel through time, fighting evil bulls from the future and keeping history on the right track . . .

When Professor McMoo invents a brilliant TIME MACHINE, he and his friends are soon attacked by a terrifying TER-MOO-NATOR – a deadly robo-cow who wants to mess with the past and change the future! And that's only the start of an incredible ADVENTURE that takes McMoo, Pat and Bo from a cow paradise in the future to the SCARY dungeons of King Henry VIII . . .

It's time for action. **COWS IN ACTION.**

READ ALL THE

COWS IN ACTION

ADVENTURES!

COMING SOON!

IF YOU CAN'T TAKE THE SLIME – DON'T DO THE CRIME!

THE SLIME SQUAD VS THE FEARSOME FISTS

BY STEVE COLE

Plog, Furp, Zill and Danjo aren't just monsters in a rubbish dump. Together they are the **SLIME SQUAD** – crime-busting super-monsters, here to save their whiffy world!

Trashland is in trouble. Fierce and fearsome fist-creatures are on the rampage, robbing banks and causing panic. Only four brave and slightly slimy monsters can possibly stop them . . . Are they up to the challenge? Or will the Fists flatten them and rule over all with an iron hand . . ?

JOIN THE SLIME SQUAD ON MORE
OF THEIR MISSIONS . . .